Demon Daddy

THE CHANGELING'S FAERIE PRINCE

KD ELLIS

ENTWINED PUBLISHING

The Changeling's Faerie Prince
ISBN # 978-1-80250-711-9
©Copyright KD Ellis 2024
Cover Art by Kelly Martin ©Copyright December 2024
Interior text design by Entwined Publishing
Published by Enchant, an Entwined Publishing imprint

Published in 2024 by Entwined Publishing, United Kingdom.

Entwined Publishing is a division of Totally Entwined Group Limited.

Entwined Publishing books by KD Ellis

Out in Austin
Teddy's Truth
Shiloh's Secret
Trusting Tennyson
Loving Lennox

Demon Daddy
The Blood Demon's Pet
The Blood Demon's Collar
The Changeling's Faerie Prince

Collections
Sold to the Billionaire: A Light at the End

THE CHANGELING'S
FAERIE PRINCE

Dedication

To Lydia Rice,
whose eyes have been invaluable,
this novel would have floundered without you
(as would have the author).

Chapter One

Rory

I remember her as she was — the blood-red berries hanging heavy from her branches, her knots of May ripe for picking. Now, her boughs are heavy and limp, weighed down by shoots blighted with purple cankers. Once-green growth is black, scorched as if by fire.

The May-tree is dying.

Her roots are gnarled, spreading across the dry earth like outstretched arms, pleading for aid that will never come. My faerie guards ignore her, shoving me past with a heavy hand.

How many lovers has she sheltered in her shadow through the endless summer? How many nights has she stood solitary, a lonely guard against the creeping winter? I feel her sorrow. It scrapes along my skin like brambles.

"What ails her?" I ask, craning my head to keep her in sight. The guard behind me — Marik, he goes by, though I remember him as Anik—slaps the side of my head, breaking my gaze.

"Walk," he orders, not deigning to give me an answer. Obstinate to the last, I set my jaw and freeze in place. His next shove sends me to my knees in the cracked dirt. "Your stubbornness will bring you only pain, changeling." Marik spits the word out like a curse, but it falls empty on my ears.

I know what I am—and what I am not.

No longer am I a mere changeling, an auf good for nothing but the breaking of skin. I am more and less. A different sort of monster, thanks to the ill-fated ritual I'd concocted out of madness and daydreams. A gossamer hope that left me too broken to live but too stupid to die.

I flash my sharp teeth and something close to unease crosses his face, a fleeting expression that sticks in my mind for longer than it lasted. He cannot hear the May-tree's screaming and cannot feel her sorrow, but I'll be damned if I let him ignore me.

"I like pain," I muse aloud, allowing myself to linger in old memories. I hadn't when they'd held me down and broken my body with lashes from the willow tree and river rock and ash, but that was before.

Before the ritual that changed everything, that twisted my body into this new, wretched thing and carved slivers of sanity from my mind. Now, I crave pain. No heroin addict has ever lusted for a needle like I for a blade.

Again, the faerie bastard looks uneasy, but Marik grips me by my hair and uses it to shove me forward. The crabgrass snags at my palms, coarse and prickly. I grind my hands into the bite.

"Then crawl, else she sends the hounds."

Ah, the hounds. Once, I'd raced them and lost. Even now, I can feel their hot breath on my neck like mountain fire. The scars have faded, but the memories are fresh, unlocked as they were by a single, careless brush of a faerie prince's hand.

I start to move but slowly. I'm in no hurry to reach the Queen's bower. I'm not scared of the pain that waits for me, but of the Queen's cunning mind, sharper than any blade she could level on my skin.

It takes us hours. Then again, maybe it costs us days. Time means little in this world-outside-the-world. A flower could bloom for a thousand years but a tree sprout up in the length of a yawn. A single night's sleep could send a harper home to a wife long dead and children grown to elders or send a bard back in the flicker of a candle.

The grass turns to cobbles, cold and sweaty with a sticky dew, and the cobbles to a smooth black path of solid pitch. It is hot against my skin, sucking in the heat from the dual sun, and the grass along its border is wrinkled and brown. We must be near the castle, but nothing is familiar. Before, the path was flowers and stone, not this mockery of pavement.

Marik plants one of his boots on my calf, freezing me in place. A voice above me — a guard, I realize as I crane my head up, just far enough to spot the supple leather of his knee-high boots — sounds amused as he says, "What have we here? A bitch returned to its master?" *Anwynn,* I realize, recognizing the voice, though I know not what name he's using now.

I bare my teeth in an imitation of a growl then give a little yip. They want me scared and they want me broken. I am not foolish enough to think that I'll survive what's coming in one piece, but I won't give them the satisfaction of cowering now.

Marik grinds his boot, the heavy leather treads biting into my skin, but I ignore the pain. I've felt pain, lived and breathed it, and once I'd died in it. My body, this farce of what had once been a man, may blossom bruises and bleed like wine but it will not break by it.

"She's waiting for him."

Marik kicks me into moving and I let him. Even if I stood up and ran, where would I go? There is nowhere in this blasted realm to hide where Queen Nuala couldn't find me. The earth is her bones, the water her weeping cunt.

Unless I can make it to the Unsidhe, who have no cause to love her, I would be back in her clutches by first dawn.

But the Unseelie Court had separated itself from the Sidhe even back when I first touched these lands, still a babe in the Darrig's arms. There are rumors of Unsidhe lands — of trees so tall their branches break through the sky, their roots growing mountains, and of spectral creatures whose voices drive the living to merriment so exquisite they forget to eat, wasting away.

There's no guarantee I could reach them without a map, and even if I do, I have nothing to entreat them with. They have no cause to love me, either. They'd be just as likely to leave me wandering the thorny labyrinth that separates their Court from this one as to lend me aid.

So instead I crawl. The floor inside the gates turns to soft wood of deepest cherry, still living but sung into shape by tree nymphs and lovingly tended by the fenodyree brownies who care for the castle.

When we reach the stairs, I go to stand but a hiss from Marik sends me back to my knees again. "You had your chance to walk, worm."

I don't bother arguing. I lumber my way up the stone stairs and try not to let the seed of relief show on my face. It's slow going, taking them on all fours, and every additional second is one I'm spared the Queen's presence.

But all good things must eventually end. Soon, far too soon, we reach the Queen's white wood door. Her crest is emblazoned in solid starlight at the center, a mockery in its beauty.

The Queen's spies must alert her to our presence because her voice calls out before Marik can lift his fist to knock. "Enter." Her voice is deceptively warm, but goosebumps lift on my arms. The door creaks open untouched, even the castle a slave to her bidding.

Marik kicks me but my body is frozen, my every muscle refusing to move. Eventually, he gives up and grips my hair, tangling my curls around his fist like a leash. The pain as he drags me inside is enough to stir me from my instinctive terror and by the time he drops me like a sack of potatoes at the side of Queen Nuala's bed, I've gathered the shreds of my strength around me like a shield.

She breaks it quickly.

* * * *

Prince Aries

The brass Celtic knot sits on my desk like a beacon, urging me to pick it up. Its message is obvious — as clear as the two words my mother had penned in her own hand.

Come home, she'd written, and this is her 'or else.'

She has Rory. He may have left me all those centuries ago, may have turned into a strange, broken thing, but I know I can't leave him to her less-than-tender mercies. I reach for the pendant.

As soon as I pick it up, it burns me—hot as dragon fire against my hand. With a pained yelp, I cast it back to the desk, cursing as it rolls across the wood. Twisting my wrist, I stare at the red, swollen knot now branded into my palm.

"What devilry is this?" I mutter, shoving back from my desk and away from the cursed thing.

Even as I watch, the scarlet brand fades from my flesh but the pain remains, throbbing with heat. The door to my office bursts open, a pair of agents nearly tripping over each other in their haste to be the first to enter.

If there had been an assassin in here, they'd have finished the job and escaped long before the two were done jostling each other. I stare at them with a dry expression, trying to hide the way my heart is still racing in my chest. I can't afford to show weakness.

"Can I help you?" I ask, struggling to keep my voice bland.

"You hollered—" the first agent starts to say.

At the same time, the second blurts out, "We thought you—"

I lift a brow at their stumbling, tangled explanation. "Everything is fine," I interrupt, waving a hand toward the door. "I'm sure you have work to do." I let my voice trail off and lift a brow, leaving the second half unsaid. *Find something to do, or I'll assign a job for you.*

"Yes, Sir," they say, this time together, and they stumble back out into the hall.

"The door," I call after them, and then it's a mess as they both try to close it. However, once I am safely alone in my office once more, I return my attention to the pendant.

This time, I grab a pen and slip it through metal chain, using it to lift it off the desk. I brace myself for the magic to strike again but it seems it must be triggered by physical touch.

Nothing happens.

A twist of my wrist sends the pendant swaying, twisting back and forth, until I'm able to get a good look at its once-smooth backing. What had before been pounded brass had been replaced with an iron plate, runes carved into its bumpy surface.

No smith or jewelry maker would have used so rough a hand, and no faerie could have handled the iron by choice. This was surely an addition by Rory, though I have no clue as to his intent. If there is magic bound to it, I don't sense any now.

Is it a message for me? There's a certain irony to it, the way he turned my gift into something I could never touch.

Grabbing the empty envelope, I let the pendant fall in. I use an obscene amount of Scotch tape to seal the toxic metal inside until I can find someone to examine it.

Then, I pick up the letter again.

Come home.

It seems my mother has finally found the one thing that could draw me back to Faerie.

With a heavy heart, I pen my resignation.

Chapter Two

Rory

Old habits come back quickly, the memories swarming to the surface like a school of fish in the Hudson River — poisonous corpses tainting anything they touch.

Stay still, stay silent.

I am a statue, smiling — *her* statue, posed by her hands for her amusement. It doesn't matter that my back is screaming from holding this position, I dare not move. Even though she's not looking, I fear she will know, and I cannot bear another punishment now.

She has me poised on my right foot, toes pointed like a ballet dancer, and my other leg is being held up by the thorned, twining vines of the Alaboa tree standing tall at the center of her boudoir. Its roots have grown beneath the cracked stone floor. Its branches shadow the bed of moss that Queen Nuala is draped over.

I keep my eyes on its splintered yellow bark.

I can do nothing to block out the sounds. Marik is atop her, plunging his cock into the Queen's leaking cunt, his pained grunts mingling with her pleasured gasps. Like everything else about her, the dew that spills from the Queen's flower is acidic.

It has blistered my lips and fingers many times. I still feel the sting now.

My poor cock is red and inflamed. I heal quicker now, in this bastardized body, but that only means she can play with me more often. She'd seemed far too pleased to learn this.

Marik screams with Queen Nuala as she reaches her peak.

I hold my breath as they pant. Will she turn to me now? There's something wrong with her, something rancid beneath her porcelain skin. So different from her son's, it shimmers like starlight to his night sky. Deceptive in its beauty. She has grown more insatiable than ever during the short span of years I'd been free.

Like her son, she's a Leanan Sidhe, a faerie whose innate magic gives mortals a muse in exchange for bits and pieces of their soul — draining their life force until they wither away like husks of their former selves. The magic doesn't work on other faeries — and now, I know for certain that it no longer works on me. I can still feel the rotted tendrils of her magic digging its way under my skin for something to hook into; the intangible, slug-like tentacles are searching and searching with nothing to show for it.

It answers a question I've had for a while — whatever monster lives beneath my flesh, it stole my soul with its birth.

Marik's voice breaks the tense silence. "What if he doesn't come for him?"

I wish I could pretend to not understand who the 'he' is that they are speaking of. It's laughable, though, that they think Aries would come for me. He's never done so before, why would he now?

Back when I was still a naïve oaf, I had cried for him, *screamed* for him. Once, I'd even broken down and prayed to him…and every last plea went unanswered. He'd left me to become the faeries favorite party favor, passed around like a joint, while he went off to play hero.

"He will come," Queen Nuala replies, her words slurring together like a drunkard's.

I feel the weight of their eyes on my body. Nudity has never shamed me but under their gaze, I feel more than just exposed…I am stripped bare as a newborn. Static fills my ears, muffling her soft footsteps as she rolls off the moss and prowls toward my strung-up body.

Then, Queen Nuala stands before me, her scarlet lips twisted in a Cheshire grin. "He *will* come for you. How could he not?" She presses her palm against my chest, and it is a burning coal on my skin. "You hold the other half of his heart."

* * * *

Much later…

Four hundred and eighty-seven.

There are four hundred and eighty-seven stones on the walls of this room. They range in color from chalk gray to sienna red, and in size from smaller than my palm to bigger than a human skull. I know because I've counted them before.

It is the same. Even the little pile of pebbles in the corner is how I left it. Undisturbed, abandoned. I remember the feel of them in my fingers, their cool smooth surface, but I don't remember what I'd been trying to build. Certainly not a way out.

I strain my memory but the wrong one flickers to life, dragging me into it like an undertow. I scratch and claw but not even the pain of my shredded skin is enough to help me dig my way out of it.

I wake up slowly. The bed below me is soft, living moss topped with griffin feathers and covered in spider-silk sheets. I stretch out my hand, frowning when I meet not the warm flesh of the faerie who bedded me the night before, but a long stretch of empty.

Someone laughs, the braying sound loud enough to startle my eyes open. I scramble for the sheets, tugging them over my nude form, and feel a scarlet heat coursing through my body. Three faerie men are standing at the foot of the bed. I look from face to face and all of them are strange.

But not unfamiliar. I may have been born in a foreign land called Tela-mon, but this is my home. My life has been bound to Prince Aodhan's. As he ages, so I age – a forever companion, his whipping boy. And now, his lover. I know the faces of these faeries. Never did I think I would wake in Prince Aodhan's bed surrounded by them.

Nearest the door stands Alberich, and farthest stands his twin, Anwynn. They are light and dark – Alberich with his black hair and pale skin and Anwynn with his golden flesh and hair the color of goldenrod. Pranksters, the both of them.

At the center is Anik, the eldest of the trio by three nights. His face is familiar most of all. Prince Aodhan's perpetual shadow. Always whispering in my prince's ear, the voice behind the meanest of his childhood pranks. Not that all of them could be laid at his feet. The elfknots were commonplace by now, I'd been waking up with them for as long as I can remember.

I lift my hand, feeling the small tangle right behind my ear.

"Where is Prince Aodhan?" I ask, and even in memory my voice is weak.

Anik laughs.

No, the laughter is real, I realize as the memory loosens its hold on me. Anik — Marik, he goes by now — is leaning against my closed cell door as I come back to myself, his lips twisted up and stained by his laughter.

My body is kneeling at the center of the stone cell, a keening cry leaking from my dry, cracked lips until I choke it off. My cheeks are now, like then, wet with an embarrassment of tears. That memory — the one single night spent in Aodhan's arms — was one of the first I'd locked away when I learned the spell to do so.

Aries, I remind myself. *He goes by Aries.*

He may have a new name now, but he is the same bastard as before.

Queen Nuala seems to believe that he harbors some feeling for me, that taking me from Earth a second time and dragging me to Faerie will draw him home, but she's mistaken.

He abandoned me then, and he'll abandon me now.

I can't hold out hope that Aries will rescue me. If I let myself play the role of damsel, the Queen won't be the only one disappointed. My breath is ragged as I push myself to my feet, swaying as I face Marik with clenched fists raised.

I have no hope of winning against the faerie warrior. Anik — the same silver-haired faerie who'd dragged me out of Aries' bed and into Queen Nuala's — was a swordsman beyond compare even then. I don't think his skill has lessened with his name change. He's had centuries more to hone his craft in the time I've been away.

He swats my hands down with ease before I can land a strike, then forces me back to my knees. I feel my inner monster trying to escape but I fear it—the creature born from the failed ritual that I'd attempted all those years ago—more than I fear the swordsman. It's a grotesque thing, a strange melding between man and faerie and demon.

"Good morning, little flame," Marik mocks. He curls his hand around my throat and laughs when I struggle. His hand is too tight on my neck. It seems all the strength I thought I'd forged in my time on Earth has fled from me, for I feel as weak as I did all those years ago.

Marik holds up a purple flower. The bulb is long and slender, the petals flared at the tip. Something in the back of my head whispers a warning—I've seen it before, even if I don't remember. The faerie lifts it to my lips but I keep them clamped shut.

I don't know what will happen if I eat it, but I do know that it would be something terrible.

"You always did fight it at first," Marik murmurs, his voice all the more chilling for its gentleness. "Open up, little rabbit. Let me make you feel all better."

Nothing could make me feel better, not with the phantom hands still pinching and poking and prodding, not with *her* stench still on my skin. Not in this place, this horror masquerading as a daydream.

But Marik clearly remembers more of this place than I do. While I know I don't want the flower anywhere near me, I don't know how to fight him off, and he seems to anticipate every move that I try to make.

Then, once he has me on my back with a knee to my chest, he uses his free hand to grip my face, squeezing until I have no choice but to unclench my jaw or break it.

Break it, I tell my body, but my body doesn't listen. My mouth opens on its own, letting out a pained gasp just before he shoves the flower inside. It tastes of mint and even before I swallow, I can feel a fog creeping into my mind, numbing the memories and the fear, until I don't remember why I don't want to swallow. Why wouldn't I want it? The flower tastes of happy things...and who wouldn't want that?

My mind goes empty and my voice goes quiet and for the first time in a long time, everything in the world feels right.

Chapter Three

Prince Aries

As I pace the sidewalk outside the Essex County Medical Examiner's office, I wonder how my mother had expected me to 'come home'. The destruction of the Bureau's primary headquarters in Old York brought with it the death of the only government-sanctioned portal to Faerie.

Even if the BAA could get it operational again — a big if, and something that will likely take years, if not decades — I had handed in my resignation. I can't just pop in and beg access.

However, there is a second portal. It's run by an elfling right here in Newark. Several of our agents have been monitoring the storefront for a few years. Director Graves had thought — and I'd agreed — that it would be best to leave it be. As long as we knew where it was, we could keep track of who was coming and going. It isn't difficult to catch up with the undocumented migrants later and impress upon them the importance of completing the proper paperwork. If we shut it down, it would inevitably reopen somewhere else, possibly somewhere outside our ability to surveil.

If I am going to approach the elfling, I will need payment. I know from our interrogations that he doesn't take anything so plebian as cash, which means a trip to the Burrows.

And a trip to the Burrows means a separate payment for its guardian, one I am loath to collect.

Hence my uncomfortable pacing outside the morgue.

As soon as I see Dr. Armitage leave for her lunch — right on time, it seems my bribe paid off — I stride up the sidewalk and stare at the doorknob. There's not enough iron in the lock for it to ignore my magic's urge to let me in. A few seconds later, I hear the *click*. The door sighs open. I slip through and close it gently behind me.

Immediately, I start to shiver. It's not the first time I've visited a morgue. It's not even the first time I've done so less than legally. I'm used to the chill that permeates the air but not the oppressive silence.

I feel Death in the shadows.

I ignore the weight of her gaze and take the stairway down to the basement. I knew what to expect — I'd heard the reports myself, seen the casualties on the streets — but the number of bodies still manages to catch me off guard. One waits on every table and in every cubby, and a jumble of parts is mounded on the counter, set aside, I'm guessing, to be sorted for identification.

The doctor's not bothering with autopsies — regardless of the cause of death, I know that they will all be attributed to my friend — to *Leviathan's* — escape. From the array of bodies, I believe the doctor is simply striving for identification before the corpses are taken away for mass burial.

There's a plot outside the city waiting.

There's something truly horrifying to me about the plan to bury the dead in the bones of an old amusement park.

I bury my worry and shove down my queasiness as I pull out a dagger. I stare at the youngest body in the room, so small I suspect she'd still been in nappies, and turn away. I cannot convince myself to mutilate her further, dead though she may be. I settle on the body of a young man instead. Perhaps he'd been old enough to work.

His blood stinks as it coats my fingers.

I keep carving.

* * * *

Despite the change in location, the gateway to the Burrows is exactly as I remember it. I'd last entered it through the wobbly stall door of a subway bathroom. Now, it has relocated to the alley between a hair salon and a dispensary. I wrinkle my nose against the smell, that sweet stale stench of pot and peroxide. It makes my skin crawl. I don't understand how the Blanks can inhale the first into their bodies or paint the second onto their hair.

The circle of mushrooms doesn't seem bothered by the foul air. It's thriving, sprouting up in the cracks of the pavement — they might look soft and pretty but, like so much of Faerie, it's deceptive. I would hazard a bet that prior to the entrance appearing here, this pavement was strong and smooth. It still has the deep black shine of one freshly sealed.

Whoever paid for this is going to be livid when the gateway moves and the Burrows' glamour fades.

The Burrows is neither here nor there, caught halfway between Faerie and the mortal realm, and outside the laws of both. For that reason and others, many of my kind have become frequent visitors. Even the Blanks have stumbled across it on occasion. I've heard them call it "going under hill."

To me, it feels like going home…but just like home, it can be deadly.

I step over the ring. Immediately, the stench of sweet weed dissipates. If I close my eyes, I could pretend to be in a meadow, and I can almost hear the faint rushing of a nearby stream.

For a second, I let my mind clear, abandoning my fear for Ruari — *Rory* — and my distaste at going home, and allow myself to just…exist. I feel weightless, like I've snipped my tethers and am floating away. Then the sound of sirens in the distance breaks through the glamour and I retreat back into my body.

This is why Faerie circles can be dangerous. It takes only seconds for them to enchant you. For every mortal who makes it into the Burrows, another three get trapped in the siren song, losing themselves to the peace while the world moves on without them.

Sighing, I force myself back to reality and sit down, cross-legged, at the center of the circle. I examine the mushrooms around me.

There are black trumpets and buttons, and goldstalks and milkcaps. Yellow blushers tangle with black knots, and a boggy brittlegill peeks out beneath an old-man-of-the-woods. So many to choose from. There's even a destroying angel hiding behind a slippery jack.

I'm about to snag a devil's finger when I spot a wood blewit. Of all the varieties that grow here, it's my favorite. Not only is it lovely with its purple suede cap, iridescent edges, and lavender gills, but it has a much better texture than its slimier cousin.

The mushroom tastes like candied dirt. Nothing like the sweets that the castle brownies used to bake it into. No matter how many times I've sampled it, for some reason it always catches me by surprise.

As soon as I swallow, I feel myself falling through the pavement into the cool dark. I hold my breath until I land, crouched, on solid stone. Before I can exhale, the Burrow's guardian steps out of the shadows.

The Luricawne is strange to me, though I know who he is from his lurid red coat. It's old, crafted from the furs of a long extinct beast and dyed a brilliant crimson that's faded in patches around his narrow shoulders. Faerie lights glint across the seven rows of seven buttons that keep it clasped shut.

I've never seen one of his kind without it. Some have claimed that he is the only one left, and each of us simply meets a new facet on each visit. It would explain how each knows the bargain I've made with the last.

It matters not to me so long as he guides me fairly through the labyrinth. Though I suppose I might regret his passing after the fact, since without him all the treasures my kind has buried here would be lost to these warrens.

"Payment?" the Luricawne demands, his voice gritty. When he bares his teeth, they are jagged and sharp. Despite his short stature, I feel the urge to step back. The Blanks may see only his glamour — a round faced, bearded man with red cheeks and twinkling eyes — but my gaze goes deeper to the skeletal, hungry creature beneath with his many shifting faces.

I dig into my pocket for the Ziploc bag and hold it out, grimacing at the coppery smell leaking through the seal. He takes it from me and sniffs the plastic.

"Barely young enough," he gripes, but tucks the bag out of sight.

I'd struggled enough with this one. It is enough to solidify my thought that it is time to empty my treasure in full. My first visit, I'd needed to give him only a freshly cut clump of hair, the second a tooth. Each visit it seems that the price is getting steeper, and eventually I know that I'll hesitate to pay.

"This way," the Luricawne gestures to the gaping archway behind him, then turns on his heel to step into the shadows. "Stay on the path."

His shoes click on the stone. I follow at a distance, careful to keep him in sight as we enter the labyrinth. In my youth, I'd been unafraid here in the inky dark, certain that no one could best me in a fight and nothing could catch me against my will. I'd been brave then…and stupid.

The air grows chilly. Goosebumps lift on my skin and I find myself rubbing my arms, following closer to the Luricawne as I peer into the darkness behind each turn we don't take.

At least I can still find my way out. We took the first left, then the second right, then the first left…or was it the second? And then…had it been a right, the last time? I shiver and stop for a second, peering behind me.

The path is gone, swallowed by a thick, gray fog. If I look close enough, I swear I see faces forming, laughing soundlessly at me. I spin around and swallow. For a second, I am alone in this terrible dark. Then the Luricawne emerges from an archway to the right.

"Stay on the path," he orders.

"The path is gone," I explain, gesturing behind me. Had it disappeared like this on my last visit? I strain my memories, but everything feels dim and flat with blurred edges. I remember the Luricawne with sharp clarity—that one had been blond with ringlets and laugh lines and, as always, his lurid red coat—but not the labyrinth. "I was just—"

"What do you think happens," the Luricawne interrupts, his face blank, "to those left behind?"

Nothing good, I think, and resolve to stick closer to his heels.

"This way," he says, gesturing toward the path on the right. I follow him through the archway, forcing myself not to turn around.

Soon I start to hear noises in the distance. Faint at first, so quiet I think I'm imagining it. At first, I think it's the yowling of a cat, then a baby's cry.

"*Aodhan?*" Someone calls out the name of my childhood, and I freeze.

"Rory?" I call out into the distance, my feet turning toward the dark opening to my left. Had the sound come from this way? I step toward the curved stone arch, straining my ears. The Luricawne's footsteps fade away.

"Rory?" I call again, and I think I hear an answer.

He sounds scared and soft, a combination so foreign I find myself filled with fear. What has she done to him to break his stubborn spirit so quickly? Or has time in Faerie passed quicker, leaving him to think I've abandoned him?

Now I'm beneath the curve of the arch, eyes straining to see through the shadows. My heart pounds as I listen. Closing my eyes, I catch a familiar scent. Sickly sweet, like death and sex and rotting meat.

Hawthorn. The May-tree...

I'm lifting my foot to follow the smell of home when a heavy hand grips my shoulder, yanking me back. The Luricawne growls, the sound deep and angry. "You faeries are always more trouble than you're worth." He shoves me away from the archway, which I notice has suddenly fallen silent. No hint of hawthorn remains. Instead, all I smell is dampness and rot.

"What's down there?" I ask, heart thudding in my chest with a fear I've never felt before. It presses on my skin and seeps down into my bones.

"Nothing that concerns you, unless you'd like to join her for dinner," the Luricawne answers and I shudder. I suspect that if I were to have continued down that path, I would have become dinner instead.

"Stay on the path."

We walk. Time, always elusive, is meaningless here. My thighs, well-conditioned from endless training with the sword and shield, start to burn, and the soles of my feet tighten and cramp. My left hip starts to ache. My jaw splits open in a wide yawn and I rub my eyes. When I open them, a glimmer of golden light catches my gaze and tugs it to the right.

Faerie lights. I haven't seen them in ages but they are as hauntingly beautiful as I remember. Iridescent, like bubbles blown by a child on a spring morning, then sparking gold like a firefly, they dance together at the center of the large domed cavern to my right.

Good luck and happy tidings they are, a sign of fortune to come. I stop and stare at their lazy patterns, drawn into a memory I'd long ago buried.

"Aodhan! Over here!" Anik — my mother's lover and my dearest friend, my shadow — calls. He is standing in a patch of second sun's light. His silver hair is cast in shades of blue and his smile is wicked. My returning grin is sharp.

I meet him next to the young oak.

"Look." Anik points to the soft brown mud. A print, or part of one. I see the curve of a heel and the start of a graceful arch. My prey went this way.

"Good eyes, Anik," I praise him, crouching down and angling my head to examine the print better. Had my little bunny slipped, or is this a false trail? I lean closer and sniff, the sound like an animal. Always, my bunny smells of sunflower sorrow. This print smells of marigold mischief.

"Smart bunny," I murmur. I twist on my heel and look in the other direction. I almost miss it. There, a snapped twig, bent unnaturally by a hurried body slipping past. "That way."

Anik, when I stand and look at him, looks angry but only for a moment. He wipes his expression clear and covers it with a laugh. Poor Anik has always been competitive – and has never been quite good enough to beat me. I suspect it's part of the reason he fucks my mother so willingly, despite the risk.

She's fickle as a summer storm and has proven time and time again that she holds no soft feelings for those who warm her bed. Too many of them end up statues in the gardens. My own father is one of them, a big bear of a faerie with a stoic face and flesh of black marble.

"Lead the way," Anik says.

I whisper an entreaty to the moss beneath my bare feet to keep my steps quiet and it softens with obedience. My approach is silent and when I see my prey, I have all the time in the universe to look.

For a moment, I am jealous of the still waters that cradle his nude body. He is floating on his back, his arms outstretched. His graceful fingers breed ripples on the otherwise calm pond. His fiery hair is a riot of color around his peaceful face. His hips dip beneath the serene surface.

Something hot kindles in my chest and burns brighter with each passing moment. He looks calm, peaceful. In this moment, there is only him and the lake and the sunlight kissing his pale, perfect skin.

I want to ruin him.

He has no right to look happy here, alone.

He has no right to feel something that has forever eluded me. Ever since my mother bound his mortal soul to my own immortal essence when I was but newly blossomed, I have craved him. When he is away, I feel…incomplete. A yawning, yearning empty in my chest, a sucking vacuum that reaches and reaches for his warmth but always comes back hollow.

But when he is near, and the empty is content, I hate him even more. I hate the hold he has on my otherwise perfect being. No other creature, mortal or fae, has such power over me. I am the strongest of my kind, the fastest with a cutting word and the most skilled with a blade. Even my mother hesitates to push me too far.

Why should this mortal, this red-haired demon in a man's form, have such sway over my countenance?

"Go back to the castle, Anik," I order.

My friend looks startled at first, then angry, but he gives a sharp bow and fades obediently back into the shadows.

I clench my fists at my side and step out of the tree line to the sandy beach. The air around me goes still and something alerts Ruari of the change. His eyes snap open and his prior calm vanishes. His face goes tense, and he sinks momentarily beneath the water. It swallows his yelp. He pops back up with a gasp a second later.

"Aodhan? How did you find me?" Ruari's voice crackles with the change from boy to man. My own does the same. He speaks quieter, as if to hide it. Though his voice is soft, I can hear his fear.

The fire still burns in my chest. So calm without me, and now that I'm here, all he feels is dread. How unfair that he gets to be peaceful when I don't.

"Silly bunny," I answer as I step to the water's edge. Crouching, I trail my fingers through the cool water. It only *takes a tendril of magic to convince the seaweed to answer my call. Green and slimy, they stretch for the hazy sunlight above them. I feel their contentment when the first vine finds one of Ruari's slender ankles.*

"I'll always find you."

Ruari's gold-flecked, green eyes widen as the plant yanks him beneath the water.

Behind me, Anik's laugh seems to echo from the forest.

The memory shatters into a thousand pieces of broken glass, piercing my flesh like daggers, and now I am the one drowning. I open my eyes and see only darkness, like the bottom of that lake I'd held Ruari under for almost too long. I still remember what he looked like when the seaweed shoved him out into my arms. The pale face, the blue lips.

It was the first time I'd ever felt fear, and when he'd woken, spewing water from his lips and tears from his eyes, I'd known a relief I'd never felt since. And for the first time, when he'd opened those pretty eyes—*how had I never known they were pretty before?*—I'd felt something else. Something foreign. *Shame.*

Now, I am the one drowning.

Pressure builds around me, painful at first before it turns to numbness. If I just close my eyes and let it take me, everything would be better. I could forget about my past and leave my worries for the future here, where they can sink into the dry, dusty dirt and grow into something beautiful.

If I just let go—

Five points of pain bite into arm and I am dragged back. I blink my eyes and slowly, the labyrinth reforms around me. The Luricawne's nails, sharp and black, are digging into the flesh of my arm, drawing beads of blue blood that slowly trickle down my skin, warm and wet.

"Thrice I have warned you, and thrice you have failed." His voice is ominous and a cold, damp sweat creeps down my spine. "A fourth time, and I will let the path take you."

He releases me and twists on his heels, his spine straight and accusing as he walks away. This time, I stick close to his shadow.

I feel a wave of relief when he turns the next corner and I spot a familiar enclave. The sylvan hilt of my sword *Teremor* rests against the stone wall, her faceted emerald pommel catching the light and glowing with it.

I hurry over and grip her hilt, a surge of heat coursing through my palm where we touch. A greeting from an old friend. "Welcome back, beauty," I murmur. My arm feels complete again, and I'm almost loath to strap her scabbard to my side if it means releasing her. She thrums with silver pleasure.

I uncover the rest of my treasures. My satchel of coins and plucked petals is easy. I hold no particular attachment to it. The rest, though…a melancholy ache grows in my stomach as I stare at them. Each and every one of them reminds me of Faerie, a place I'd long thought I'd never return.

I gather them up slowly, and each piece I add feels like returning a part of myself that I've been missing — the *féth fíada*, a cloak of mist gifted to me by a visiting threadwitch, her name long since lost to my memories; my Bow of Yearning, carved from the roots of a fallen dryad during the Age of Morrigan, when no end to the war between Courts was in sight; my boots of wander, which make no sound.

I don them all and only hesitate on the last. My Circlet of the Woodland Hart, the symbol of my rank and authority. Carved from the antlers of the Golden

Stag, plated in silver and adorned with emeralds, once I'd been proud to bear its weight upon my head.

Now, I feel a strange blending of shame and sorrow. It rides heavy on my skull.

From the cool dark, a breeze begins to trickle. Quiet at first and slow, the eddies sluggish, but then it strengthens, swirling around my boots and kissing my skin. Soon, it tickles my neck, bringing with it the memory of a far-off place and a warning. Unease swirls in my belly as my cloak flutters.

Suddenly, I wonder how long I've been gone. When I'd left Faerie, I hadn't meant it to be permanent. It hadn't even been planned—a gateway had opened in front of me and on a whim, I'd stepped through, willing to do anything to escape the scars of war and the memories of Ruari.

Everywhere I'd looked, I'd seen remnants of him—his red hair in the petals of the spirea bushes that lined the path of my garden; his pale blue eyes in the waters of my favorite pond; his warm flesh in every patch of golden sunlight.

Not even the War of the Courts had been enough to erase him from my mind; it just opened wounds of its own.

So the Tear had opened, and I'd stepped through. How many faeries had I mocked for doing the same? The doorways between worlds opened on a whim, or so it had seemed at the time. It would open once on each sunrise on one day, and then not again for the lifespan of a hare, and then open thrice more in the space of a breath. Unpredictable and dangerous—a faerie who chose to visit the mortals might return the next morning, or not for a hundred thousand sunsets.

Once I'd crossed through, the cause of the unpredictability had been obvious. Random in Faerie because it *wasn't* random on the mortal plane…it opens every fifty years and stays open from the first drop of sunlight to the last and not a second more.

I've been on Earth through the opening of eight Tears. We don't track time in Faerie, not like the mortals do here. We track it in the blooming of the Ethylas flower and the growth of mountains.

As of the opening of the last Tear forty years ago, relations between the Sidhe and Unsidhe were uneasy but nonviolent. And obviously, my mother is still alive and thriving in her rule. It is the smaller things that I wonder about.

I fear what might have happened in my absence. It is a dread like quicksand, slow and inexorably growing. It takes me too long to realize that the fear isn't mine, it's coming from somewhere else. My skin grows icy and then I hear it—a prickle-pained plea.

Faerie is crying.

Chapter Four

Rory

"Lilies, lilacs, lavender and laudanum," I singsong as I wander the hedgerows. The Queen — *Queen of Cards, the eater of hearts, of men and monsters and rotted parts* — banished me from her bedchamber sometime between the rising of the first sun and the second.

I'd found myself in the smallest of the royal gardens. It feels familiar and if I close my eyes, I can almost hear the flowers welcoming me home. I dance between the raised beds, trailing cold fingers — *so cold, why am I always so cold?* — over prickly stems and velvet petals.

"Mistletoe, merrigolds and the myrtle, maudlin."

Leaning down, I pluck a black berry, plump as a cherry and doubly sweet, and plop it in my mouth. It stains my skin with purple juices. My fingers look like they've been dipped in violet ink.

Paint, splattered across golden skin — a brief memory surfaces before it's numbed away.

"Sassafras and sugarplums, and sunflowers slumbering. Yet nevermore the garden grows, when the sky is mumbling."

"That's a pretty song," someone with a deep voice — *a familiar stranger, a threatening danger* — says from behind me. I don't startle.

"Hm-mmm? Song?" I turn toward the voice with a smile, mind blank and sated. "Was someone singing?" Faintly, I hear it, an echo of a melody. My fingers itch for the strings of a lute. I can feel the vibration against my skin. I hum along.

The man — *monster, faerie bastard* — gives me a crescent grin. "Poor little rabbit, still snared by the *Salvia*? It's for your own good, you know." He steps closer. His silver hair hangs over his shoulder in a loose braid. I hear it whispering. I stretch my hand out to touch but he slaps it down. The pain is sharp but fleeting.

"Marik!" I blurt his name as it comes to me, woken by the stinging pain in my hand. I frown down at it, noticing for the first time the many small cuts dotting every inch of my exposed skin.

When I look back up at the faerie, I see him doubled — the smirking man, nude and kneeling at the Queen's feet, and the cold man standing stern in the shadow of a dying May-tree. Then I blink and the images fade away.

There is just me and Marik in the garden.

"There you are, rabbit." Marik's smile turns sharp. "Do you remember?"

"Remember?" I repeat, pain creeping behind my eyes as I struggle to think.

Fog-phantom images dance through my mind — *a world of electric lights and smog-choked streets; women with knees bared to the air and wary eyes; Aodhan, my prince of war, with a breadth of shoulder I'd never seen before.*

"Are my dreams memories? Or are my memories only dreams?" I ask, deadly serious, but Marik just laughs. The sound strikes me from all angles, sharp as shattered glass. It leaves invisible wounds in my skin.

"Asked and answered," Marik says, voice quiet, as if to himself, and then he pulls a pretty, purple flower from his pocket. "A treat for you, rabbit," he says and holds it out.

Disquiet in my chest, I take it with obedient fingers that shake and eat it, ignoring the small voice crying in the back of my mind. Mint stings my lips and almost immediately, my thoughts of a strange world grow dim. There is only here and only now.

"On your knees, little one," Marik says as he opens the ruby robes of his *hanfu*, exposing a swath of pale skin.

Ivory on my lips and
Salt on my tongue
Thistles in my skin and
Brambles in my bum.

I snicker as the silly poem blooms in my head, distracting me from the goings-on around me. Will-o-wisps dance behind my eyelids and tickle my cheeks and I hear myself laughing. I open my eyes and see a little person in the glimmer.

It is Aodhan-now-Aries, standing stiff with a heavy frown in a cavern deep beneath the ground. A crown of antlers and emeralds sits on his brow and a breeze twists violently around him. It sings to him my pain. His lips twist down just as I swat him away, cursing him for abandoning me. I feel caught somewhere between never and now.

Had he bedded me last night or never?

A large white hand grabs my wrist and presses it into the dirt.

My body stops moving. The thistles crunch beneath footsteps as Marik leaves. I stay behind, safe in *Salvia* dreams. The grass grows beneath my chest and when it gets too prickly, I roll to my back and stare at the sky.

It turns to star-speckled black, then the hazy violet of predawn. I watch the first sun rise with its golden glow, then the cerulean second, and they dance together across the sky before slumbering together in the darkness, then they dance together again, and again.

My belly grumbles a protest, but I don't move to feed it. Instead, I watch the two lovers in the sky and let myself dream. Someone had held me once, hadn't they? Stroked my skin with gentle hands and brushed lips like burning coals over my flesh? I close my eyes and try to remember his face. I get a glimpse of dark skin and eyes lit with amusement before the *Salvia* blurs it away into nothing.

Then Marik is back, frowning down at me. His *hanfu* is orange now and his hair looks longer. Suddenly, I feel hungry. I offer him a smile and his frown deepens.

"Have you been here all this time, rabbit?"

I laugh. "What is time?"

Chapter Five

Prince Aries

The trip out of the Labyrinth is simple. The Luricawne leads me in a straight line past three turn offs then we step through the archway into the main chamber. The Faerie circle waits. The mushrooms dangle from the low stone ceiling. They glow a faint teal now.

The Luricawne is solemn as I face him. He watched me strip my treasures from the mound and garb myself in them like a soldier being outfitted for war. He knows I am not returning. I tense, waiting for anger or threats, but the creature is stone-like, his face blank.

"If you change your mind, you know where to find me. The cost will be a bird with a broken wing."

I would not change my mind. I feel the shroud of prophecy draping itself over me like a cowl. It is a heavy weight on my shoulders and suddenly I know that I will make it to Faerie but never see this world again.

I close my eyes against the pain of the realization. I think I've always known it and that's why I've avoided going home for so long. I like this world, with its ever-changing politics and thrill of danger. Never knowing what waits around each corner, having to wade through lies to find the truth. And, best of all...the hole inside me that I'd felt ever-present in Faerie had not followed me through the veil to this world.

For the first time in my existence, I'd felt...complete, or nearly. I'd still missed Ruari's presence, but it was the difference between a toothache and a hangnail. Without him, I'd never be truly whole.

As a faeling, young and naïve, I'd been angry at Ruari for that fact. Punished him, over and over, for the way he made me feel. When I'd realized my mistake that fateful day by the pond's edge, I was almost too late. He'd looked at me with distrust for long after that. Well after his voice had smoothed out into the youthful baritone and he lost his childhood lankiness.

From a bunny he'd grown into a gazelle, and still he'd feared me. It was my fault, I know that now. He'd had no reason to trust my sudden change of heart. No reason to suspect that the lack of elfknots in his hair was not a new trick of mine to lull him into placidity before I started a new prank.

I shove down the pain and give the Luricawne a small nod. Then, I step into the Faerie circle. I stretch to pluck a mushroom and eat it with a promise. When I find Rory, it will be different. I feel the circle pull me upward, through stone and steel and sorrow, then I am kneeling on the warm pavement in the foul-smelling alley again.

The Burrows fades away, but my vow remains.

This time, I won't fail him. He may have fled my bed last time, but not again. This time, I'll do better. This time, I'll earn his trust *and* his love.

I just have to get to Faerie first.

* * * *

"What do you mean, closed?" I cross my arms as I stare down at the elfling standing between me and my way back to Faerie. Not home. It hasn't been home in a long time.

"Closed. Shut down. Not working. Expired. Temporarily disconnected. Malfunctioning. Gone hayw—" the elfling says, his voice bored and dull. Despite that he only comes up to my knees, he shows no fear. Behind him, the normally bright portal is dull and static. A circle of plain stones on the thirsty brown grass.

Now that he's said it, I can feel the difference in the room. I've only used a private portal once but that time, I could feel the magic—electric, like I was holding onto a powerline. I remember the way the plaster walls had seemed to quiver with it, the foggy tendrils of crackling energy obscuring the tall ceiling like storm clouds. This room is still. If not for the rune-carved stones, I would think that I'm in the wrong place.

"For how long? It's imperative that I get back to Faerie at once." I'm trying to stay calm but without this doorway, I'm stuck here until the next gateway opens on its own. What is my mother doing to Rory even now as I waste time here? My skin crawls at the thought.

"Unless you have a spare Janus key and lock plate, you—like everyone else—will have to wait." The elfling dares to turn his face from me. I bristle at the insult and fight the urge to grab his chin and force him to look back. Instead, I draw in a calming breath. I am no longer the same hotheaded prince from Faerie. I have had time — so much time, *too* much time — to learn to be better.

I swallow, ridding my voice of daggers, and speak. "You are a Keeper of the Door. If anyone knows a way into Faerie, I trust it would be you."

The elfling looks back, his gaze considering. "You are the first to ask, so I will tell you true. There are only three ways that I know of that may be of help to you."

"I'm listening," I say.

I sense him wrap his riddle around his body as he starts to speak. "Of those who guard the way between, there are only four besides your Queen. Myself, I run this doorway fair. I charge a price and square is square. But that which broke I cannot fix until the moon has cycled six."

Six months until this doorway would be operational. Six months too long.

"The second Keeper I would not trust for as long as the glaciers glisten with frost. His name is Ember and his hate runs deep. No faerie I've met has survived the meet."

Ember...I shudder at his name. I know of him, though he'd been banished from Faerie long before I'd blossomed. He was one of us, once. A Seelie warrior, the best in my mother's honor guard...until something went awry. Every story was different...some said he cast a spell that backfired, some said it was an Unsidhe curse, some said he'd always been broken. Whatever truly happened, it twisted him into an ugly, mangled thing.

Part faerie, part...something else. No longer weakened by iron and salt, he'd lured hundreds of my kind to their death during the Slaughter. In the end, he'd killed so many that both Courts had put aside their differences to cast him out. It was the only time in Faerie history that I've ever heard of my mother and the Unseelie King working together.

No, Ember would not look favorably on a faerie asking safe passage.

"Third brings danger, that is true, but perhaps less so for a swordsman like you. Look under the M-Bridge for a troll named Graf. Survive his hunger to find the path."

I wrinkle my nose and hope the fourth way is better. I don't love trolls. Besides the fact that they are stupid as rocks, they always reek. I've yet to find one who hadn't turned pristine waters into a bog.

"Last but not least, go to Hammond and find, at the Djinn and Tonic, a centaur kind. Lynilsa will help you if you pay the right cost. A typical charge is a memory's loss."

Memory magic...powerful and dangerous, but likely my best shot.

The riddle fades and the elfling turns toward the door again. "Now go, little prince. It's nearly noon. I have a date with a gnome to get to soon."

And I need to get to Hammond. I'd happily sacrifice a memory—I have too many that I'd happily trade— than parley with a troll.

I leave the little shop and step back onto the sidewalk, resolved. Unfortunately, my determination wanes quickly when I think about the details of the trip. I can't just hop on my bike and go. Maybe I could have, if it was centuries ago, but it's not. I would run out of petrol long before I found a fill-up station, and that's if the iron sickness doesn't strike me first. I've padded it well enough for short trips around the city, not a half-day trip up the broken interstate.

I stop outside a random shop and stare up at the sky while I think. I could unstable Arion. It has been a while since we'd had a good ride together, though I know he gets plenty of love and affection from the mortal who boards him. Mae had been raised with him, after all. Six generations of her family had cared for my steed since I'd emigrated from Faerie.

But taking Arion will mean sticking close to water for the whole journey, and that might slow me down.

I rub my thumb and forefinger together as I think, the repetitive motion a force of habit. More and more people had taken to horseback as a mode of transportation. Bicycles are great for the city but not so great for long distance, and cars are unreliable. If I were still employed with the Bureau, I'd fly, but private flights—especially faerie safe ones—are expensive. Even though I can afford one, I don't remember Hammond being large enough to support an airport.

Horseback it is. I flag down a passing taxi-carriage and climb into the back. For a steep fee, he agrees to take me to Honeyridge. As the carriage starts to move, I close my eyes and think of Faerie—and of Rory, waiting.

I'm coming, Rory.

Chapter Six

Rory

The Queen is beauty incarnate. She's stolen thousands of poets from their beds to write of it — her hair so white it glows like starlight, her skin as pale as fallen snow, her twilight eyes. Their failures are immortalized with their bodies throughout the castle.

One only needs to look carefully at the furniture she's decorated the castle with. There is the man in her mirror. I can see him from my place on her bed, his face twisted with fear in the copper frame.

Most of the time, I can ignore them, but never the man in the mirror. There's something about his closed metal eyes, the way his fingers curve, clenched, around the bottom near the base. Unlike the others, the man in the mirror still seems alive.

Unlike the others, the man in the mirror makes me fear.

When she'd stolen me from my cradle, how close had I been to ending up a piece of art on her wall? What had made her tie my life to Aodhan's instead? The stolen poets weren't the only people she'd twisted like this. There were bards remade into instruments in the ballroom when their voices turned bitter, and sheep herders turned into tables, and babes frozen in time and left to line the castle walls, crying out when disturbed from sleep by trespassers.

In so many ways, she could have broken me differently.

Sometimes, I wonder what it would be like to be a mirror.

Later, after the Queen has kicked me out, I think of going to the garden.

Don't, a small voice whispers to me. *He'll find you there.*

"Who?" I ask aloud, and nearby a brownie laughs.

"Who, who," she mocks. "Poor thing, poor batty boy. He thinks he's a bird."

I ignore her and continue walking. Not toward the garden this time, but toward the kitchen. I remember — it's vague, like staring through a rain-soaked window — a cook once who'd been kind to me. A kobold who'd been only as tall as my waist but had a kind smile and a matronly face. Her name was Penny.

The *Salvia* is wearing off, I realize, as the fog at the edge of my vision starts to dissipate. The world sharpens — painfully, unfortunately, but the agony helps me focus.

I remember this feeling.

I open my eyes in the middle of a hard black river. Like water frozen, but it's hot to the touch and rough. Loud noises are blaring at me and people are yelling — so many people, more people than I could ever have imagined existed in the whole world.

I clamp my hands over my ears. Everything is loud and bright and full of motion. Someone grabs at my arm and I flinch away, but there's someone over there too. All around me, I'm surrounded by beings with round ears and red faces.

"Jesus, kid, get outta the street!"

"Are you crazy? You're going to get killed!"

They keep yelling, speaking in strange words that seem familiar but the accent is thick and wrong. I push myself to my feet and look frantically around. There, a dark narrow space between two – Gods, are those buildings? They are too large to contemplate, nothing like the small cottages the faeries love, larger by far than even the Queen's castle.

I hadn't planned to walk through the gateway when it opened, but it had been so close and so easy. I'd just…stepped through into whatever world this is. Nothing green, nothing growing…all sharp angles and cold dark. A glance up – I get dizzy as I see how high the monstrous buildings really are – reveals only a single sun.

"Where am I?" I ask in terrible wonder.

"The middle of the fucking street, you idiot!" Someone yells and another someone plants their hand in my back, shoving me toward a stretch of gray hardness lining the black. "Get on the sidewalk!"

The black river is a street…the gray stream is a sidewalk. I try to fix the two words in my mind as I stumble onto the…sidewalk…with the rest of the people. I look around me again.

There are so many people walking in so many directions…but on the gray 'sidewalk,' I realize. And the black street has gigantic, fast-moving monsters. Their legs move in circles, rolling like a stone down a hill but all together to keep the monsters in motion. And inside the monsters, there are…people?

Not monsters. Carriages…horseless carriages, moving as if by magic. So…the streets are for carriages, and the *sidewalks are for people...except where the two white lines stretch across the black street between two sidewalks? Because people seem to be walking there too...*

It's confusing and I feel frightened but before I can do more than think about asking one of the round-eared humans for help, pain stabs at my stomach like a knife. I cry out as I clutch it. My insides twist and cramp and suddenly I feel the urge to vomit. I stumble into the darkness between the two buildings, heaving.

Whatever contents it held before, I lose now, spewing it onto the grave next to a big green square box that reeked of rot.

When the vomiting finally stops, I find myself shaking, too weak to move. Whimpering, I sink back against the cold hard wall.

"Where am I?"

The memory fades but the pain remains—a too familiar cramping in my belly. I don't know how long it's been since I've eaten anything but the *Salvia* flower—there is no such thing as starving in Faerie—but it's been long enough that, despite the nausea, I manage not to throw up. Instead, I curl my arm around my stomach, much like I'd done all those years ago, and continue fumbling my way to the kitchen.

With each step, my mind clears and my body shakes harder. I know now what I didn't know then—I'm going through withdrawal.

I experienced it firsthand when I first arrived on Earth and barely survived. Days spent in a cycle of vomiting, hallucinations and terrible pain. Then, I'd thought I was growing sick from being so far away from Aodhan, whose life I'd been bound to. It was that fear that had spurred me to find that occult shop, and that same fear that had convinced me to steal the old, leather-bound tome that held the spell—and then into trying the spell, despite having no discernable magic of my own and access to only half the ingredients.

In some ways, the spell worked. The cord that bound my soul to Aodhan's had certainly withered away. I can still feel its tether in my chest but it's a weak, mutated thing. Hardly worth acknowledging, most of the time. But the spell had warped me as well.

There was a monster inside me. It kept me youthful when those around me aged, kept me strong when I felt at my weakest. I spent years searching for an answer, an explanation, and the closest I found was from a Wix who'd operated his shop out of the back of a laundromat in Brooklyn.

The spell hadn't cut the tie between Aodhan and me like I'd wanted. Rather, the spell had reversed it, stealing pieces of Aodhan's faerie essence and tangling it into my soul instead. Between his magic and the time that I'd spent in Faerie, eating its food and drinking of its waters, I'd ended up caught somewhere between human and fae.

I am both and neither.

A particularly sharp cramp makes me stumble and I'm grateful when I see the door to the kitchen ahead. Hunched over and hissing between clenched teeth, I step inside.

Someone screeches by the stove. "What are you doing in—Ruari? Oh, you poor thing, poor dear." Penny, my favorite kobold, is suddenly at my side. She pushes me with warm, tiny hands over to a small, three-legged stool in the corner. I remember her fondly, so I don't correct her pronunciation of my name. Here and now, even I am not certain who—and when—I am. Maybe this is dream. Maybe everything is.

"Sit, sit. Penny will make you some ginger tea. Settle your stomach right down, it will. *Salvia,* nasty plant it is. Penny told him it was dangerous to use it so often, but does he listen? No, no one ever listens to Penny."

She grabs a bronze kettle and carries it over to the window, which she pushes open through a combination of magic — I taste its sweet molasses on the air — and elbow grease. Penny whistles and slowly, a vine drops lower, curly ends twisting until it can push a large, green leaf, bigger than Penny's whole body, through the window. The edges are furled.

As soon as Penny holds out the kettle, the tip of the leaf unfurls into a little spout. Water starts to drip off, then trickles into a steady stream. "That's enough, dear," Penny tells the plant when the kettle is full, and it furls itself up again. The leaf retreats out of the window. The vine remains for a second, waiting.

"Oh, shoo. It's not time yet, you know that," Penny scolds, and the vine wilts before slipping back outside. She slams the window closed and carries the kettle over to the fire in the corner. Carefully, she leans over the flames and hangs it on the hook to heat.

"Now, that's done. While it heats, Penny will make you a snack. You'll need it for the journey."

"Journey?" I ask, mind a bit too muddled between the pain and the nausea to follow her words.

"Well, you certainly don't plan to stay here, do you?" Penny looks at me, surprise on her wrinkled face. "Marik is surely already looking for you. Unless you *want* another dose of *Salvia*?"

"No, of course not…" I admit, frowning, but my belly protests. I suppose I hadn't thought about it, but she's right. If I stay, he'll find me and send me right back into the stupor. How long have I even been here? "But where am I supposed to go?"

"Penny won't be tricked into helping an escape, not again. No she won't. Penny certainly would never tell you to make it to the Unsidhe, no Penny would not." Penny has a mischievous glint in her yellow eyes as she smiles at me.

"The Unsidhe? How would one find them?" I ask, hoping she will answer. I'd considered it when Marik dragged me back here and discarded the idea for a reason. I wouldn't know the first place to look.

"Penny would never tell Ruari that there's a map in Marik's study, no she wouldn't. Penny knows better than to say it's hidden in the nasty faerie's quiver."

My heart sinks.

How am I supposed to break into the office of the *last* person I want to find me and escape without getting caught?

Chapter Seven

Prince Aries

The carriage lets me out at the end of the lane leading to Honeyridge. The young driver refuses to go any closer. I don't blame him. The road is barely more than patchy grass and mud, and his carriage wheels were made for city streets. I hike the strap of my leather satchel higher on my shoulder and begin the trek.

Winter has faded into spring and the afternoon sun is pleasant. I'm grateful that my Agency-issued combat boots were meant for hard wear because it takes me over a half an hour to cover the three-mile distance. I have a nice burn in my muscles when I finally spot the white farmhouse ahead.

It doesn't take long for a Border Collie to come racing toward me. Like most animals when confronted by one of the fae, whatever innate territorial protectiveness it may have had fades away. It—he, I realize once it jumps—plants his back feet and nearly knocks me over with his enthusiasm, tail wagging.

"Hello, little beastie," I say, giving him a good scratch behind the ears before I nudge him down. "Where's your mistress?"

"Oy!" A deep, gravelly voice hollers. I look up from the dog to spot a man rounding the corner of the farmhouse, his meaty hand clenching the handle of a rake. "This is private property. Best be getting along, now."

The man stalks closer. He is nearly as tall as my glamour and about as wide, with shoulders like an ox. Laugh lines mark his face around his eyes and the corner of his lips, though his expression now is stern. His gaze lingers on the sword strapped to my side.

"I'm here to see Mae," I reply.

His brows furrow with confusion. "Mae?"

For a second, I fear it's been longer than I realized. I remember her as a young girl, full of bubbly laughter and swishing floral skirts, her raven hair wild around her sun-kissed cheeks. Surely it has not been long enough for her to pass on to wherever Blanks go once their bodies have failed them?

"Oh!" His exclamation startles me as his expression clears. "You must mean Anna. I don't think she's gone by Mae in years. She's out back with the horses."

I've called her Mae — both in my head and to her — for so long, I'd almost forgot her given name is Annamae. "Anna..." I say out loud. It is strange on my tongue. "Hm." It's not that I am unused to name changes, I have had several dozen more than I could count. I just can't picture the wild child of my memories as an Anna.

"What do you want with her anyway? I've not seen your kind around here much." His fingers tighten on the wood.

I lift a brow and wonder what he means by 'my kind'. My glamour gives me rounded ears and dulls the spark in my eyes. Perhaps I don't look human enough, but I surely can't look fae?

Before I can question him, he continues. "You're one of them cosplayers, right? From the re-enactment troupe up the hill?" He gestures to the west.

It would be so much easier if I could lie. Just nod and go along with it. Instead, I chuckle and shake my head. "Not at all. I'm an…old friend."

This time, it's him who laughs, his whole face lighting up. "How old can you be? If you is a day over thirty, I'll eat my hat! Besides, I've been working this land for what feels like forever, and I ain't never seen you before." His laughter is broken by a cough and he leans on the rake like it's the only thing keeping him upright. For the first time, I realize that he's old.

I worry my lip between my teeth for a moment and try to count the years in my head. Has it been twenty? Thirty?

Surely not forty…

"I'm older than I look," I admit. "But M—Anna will remember me."

He shrugs. "If you say so. You know the way?"

"I remember," I say to him. I give the collie a final scratch and start around the house. There's a path, grass worn down to dirt from generations of footsteps.

The paint on the house is peeling. I reach out and touch it with my fingertips. It flakes away, falling like snow to the overlong grass. As I round the corner, I stare out at the fields.

They are smaller than I remember. Trees have overtaken the left field and the right, where I remember sprawling acres of land for grazing, now hosts a jagged deep pit. An excavator nearby sits idle.

The stable is where I remember it, at least, and looks to be in as good of shape as it always was. Whatever happened to Honeyridge since my last visit, it doesn't seem to have affected how they've cared for the horses.

I take a second to scan the remaining fields, finally spotting an older woman leaning against a round pen near the middle pasture. I head that way, disquiet twisting my stomach. I've been gone for too long. It's easy to forget how fast the mortals age.

She doesn't see me at first, even though she's facing my way. Her eyes, once brilliant blue, are faded but still keen as they watch the young colt in the pen. He's a yearling, much too young to ride, with long legs and a fine chestnut coat. He's a spirited one.

He's planning something. I can feel his mischief as he trots in circles around the pen, urged along by the training whip that Mae—Anna—snaps behind him when he slows. My presence has riled him up. He goes to lunge but Anna seems to read him easily, correcting him quickly, and the colt settles back into a trot.

I don't know if she hears my footsteps or just senses my presence, but Anna looks at me just as I'm about to speak. I'm struck silent by the evidence of years that have passed. It's not just her eyes that have changed. Her face is weathered from years in the sun and her once raven hair is streaked with steel. Her grip, though, is iron on the whip.

"Aaron?" she asks, straightening. Despite her age, she looks strong and able.

"Aries, now." I say, nodding in acknowledgment. The name may have changed, but I haven't. Not really. Around me, the world moves forward, shifting and growing. I never do.

"Been a while. If it wasn't for the monthly deposits, I'd have thought you forgot about us." She smiles but there's a sharpness to it.

I wince and bow my head further. "My apologies. I've been...busy." It's the truth at least, but not a full one. I could have made time to visit but I didn't. I'd gotten distracted, thrown myself into work, anything I could to keep my mind off the loneliness trying to swallow me. The death of my last lover had hit me harder than I was willing to admit. Even now, I feel shamed.

"Busy," she scoffs, but her expression gentles. "My mother warned me about you."

"Oh?" It surprises me enough that I stumble backward. Her mother had been a lovely woman named Clarabelle. We'd been friendly enough, or so I thought.

"She said she had a bit of a crush on you. Told me she spent a summer glued to your heels like a puppy." Anna pauses, then smiles. It's small but not pained. "She also told me that loving you would be like catching a firefly."

I'd never realized her mother felt anything for me but curiosity, and my shock must show on my face. "I'm sure I don't know what you mean."

"You're a pretty thing," Annamae acknowledges. She, like her mother and grandmother before her, is gifted with the Sight. They've always seen me as I am, rather than the glamour I wear like armor.

Anna continues speaking. "And keeping you would make me feel good. But just like a firefly, if we keep you too long, you'll suffocate."

"Why would your mother tell you such a thing?" I ask, genuinely wondering.

"Because I was following too closely in my mother's footsteps. She was keen enough to spot my crush early. It seems all us women of Honeyridge fall prey to it at one time or another. She didn't want me getting my heart attached to someone who was always going to leave."

I open my mouth, but she must sense what I'm going to ask. She interrupts me. "And why am I telling you this now, after all these years?" She lifts her brows and I feel my face flush. "Because it was time. Because I don't need you to excuse away your absence. I wasn't surprised when you left. No matter how I felt at the time, you never led me on. You never made promises. I don't think it even crossed your mind to."

She's right. Even though I'd thought her lovely, even though I'd acknowledged her beauty many times, never once had I considered loving her. Not with the curse that runs in my blood. A few weeks of sampling her body would not have been worth the pain of her death. She may not paint with canvas and brushes, or make melodies on the harp or piano, but she is an artist when it comes to training horses. Her steeds would have been the best in the nation — and then she'd have died young.

I still don't understand how Rory survived. Was it because my mother had tied his soul to mine? Or because of whatever magic had twisted him into something not quite human? I wish I'd had more time to speak with him, to understand. He *couldn't* be human, not and still live. Even without my curse on him, no human could have survived this long.

Anna clears her throat as she eyes me up and down, sadness plain on her face. It pulls me from my musing. "And I'm not angry about it now. You're taking Arion?"

"I must. I'm going home."

"And if he does not wish to leave?" She asks the question plainly, as if my answer does not worry her, but I can sense a deeper emotion lurking underneath it. Fear, perhaps. Or maybe bitterness? Unlike animals, humans have always been harder for me to read.

"Why would he wish to stay?" I counter, not sure yet how to answer her truthfully. My immediate thought is that it does not matter. He is my steed, bound to me in battle so many ages ago. Our contract has not changed just because a handful of years have passed.

But an equal part of me hesitates. What would I give to not have to return to Faerie? It is a choice I cannot make for myself, but for Arion...I could give him this gift if I choose. The question remains.

Anna looks at me, and I look at Anna, and neither of us speak for the longest time. Finally, she sighs. "Come and see."

I follow her back up to the house and into a warm kitchen. The walls are daffodil yellow, the floors a faded, checkered linoleum. The cabinets are the same turquoise I remember, though the formerly iron doorhandles are now brass. It looks very much as I remember it.

I go to question why we've not gone for the stables but then I spot the youthful man standing at the sink washing dishes. His hair is smooth and black as ink and pulled back in a loose braid, threaded with multicolored stone beads. He's turned away from me so I can't see his face but I recognize the deep notch near the tip of his pointed ear where it peeks out from his hair.

"Arion?" I say, letting the door swing closed behind me. Anna steps closer to the counter, her hand resting near the cutting board—and the silver butcher's knife atop it. A threat or a warning?

He stills for a long stretch of seconds, then slowly draws his webbed fingers out of the water. "Prince," he greets me, his voice deep, but there is no pleasure in it. When he faces me, his jaw is tense and his eyes are wary. A blue-and-silver beaded necklace is clasped around his throat.

Sunlight glints off his wringing hands and I glance down. There's a plain gold band on his left ring finger. It's worn with age. A glance toward Anna shows a matching one on her hand.

"I see."

"We have two sons and a daughter," Anna says, her voice warbling. "And our first grandchild on the way." Unlike Arion, who seems frozen, Anna straightens her spine as much as her advancing age will allow her. She takes a step over and places her hand on Arion's shoulder. "He has lived as a man for over half a century."

I'd known, of course, that he could take a man's form. After all, I'd met him in this form all those many years ago. I'd been half drowned, and he'd been salt sick. A fine pair we'd made.

I should tell him that it's okay, that he can stay here and live out the rest of her days. I doubt she has more than a decade or two left, hardly a blink of an eye. I open my mouth to do just that, but ice freezes my tongue.

Without him, how will I get to Hammond? Not on my own two feet, at least not quickly enough. I need a steed and few are faster than a water horse.

He must read my indecision on my face because he places his hand over Annamae's and squeezes. I can taste his fear like bitter iron. I open my mouth but

Annamae speaks before me. "You cannot have him, Prince of Faerie. My family has provided you shelter and sustenance for generations. You are in my debt."

I lower my head in deference but counter, "My debt was paid in coin and good fortune. My gratitude has made your fields bountiful and seasons soft."

She presses her lips together but cannot argue, for she knows it to be true. I turn my gaze to Arion. "Have you nothing to say?"

The kelpie immediately drops to his knees, face pained and voice full of longing as he speaks. His hand lifts to the necklace, fingers tracing the largest stone. "I beg of you, Prince. Release me from my contract. Let me stay."

"I cannot," I say, regretting the words but unable to take them back. "I need to get to Hammond. Take me there, and I'll let you return." It's a compromise, the best one I can make. I lift a hand briefly to his head. "You have my word."

"I'll go with you to Faerie," a different voice interrupts, light and sweet as birdsong, "in my father's place."

I look toward the doorway and lift a brow at the spirited young man. A riot of dark curls frames a pale face, upturned lips promising mischief. He's wearing a loose green blouse and wide bottom pants that pool on the ground, hiding his feet.

"No, Ayna." Anna hurries to the boy's side and grips his arm. "You don't know what you're saying."

"I am not a child anymore," the boy says, tearing his arm free and stepping further in the kitchen. "I don't belong here. We all know it. I'm tired of hiding."

"Sweetheart, you don't have to hide—" Anna starts to say, but the boy laughs.

"I'm a freak, Mama. Thirty years old and I look half that at best, and that's not even speaking of *these* – " He sticks out his left leg and instead of a foot, I see a hoof, polished and black. I've heard of this before – half breeds born of a faerie and a mortal, neither fully one nor the other. I cast out my senses and while I feel his magic – the boy, like his father, has an equine form hiding beneath his skin – there's no hint of glamour.

"But Ayna – " Anna looks to Arion.

Arion, though, appears thoughtful as he stares at his son. I stay quiet, waiting. Kelpies have always been...unpredictable. Mostly male, it's rare that they breed. When they do, it's even rarer for the father to stick around. The colt lives with the mother until it reaches maturity.

"This will not be a fairytale," Arion finally says. "Faerie does not abide the weak."

"I am strong enough," Ayna answers immediately.

For some reason, I believe him.

"If you change your mind, you may not return to the world you left behind," Arion cautions.

"I won't change my mind."

"Then go...with my blessing." Arion bows his head to his son, then stands. Annamae chokes on a sob and he is surprisingly gentle as he clasps her to his chest. The two couldn't look more different – her, wizened with age and sorrow, him young and strong as a warrior – but there's something intangible tying them together, two halves of a larger whole.

Arion looks over his wife's head, his expression taut. "I entrust my son to your care. Take him home, Prince."

I hesitate, eyes lingering on Annamae. Something tells me that if I take her child from her now, she will never forgive me. My welcome with her family will end, here and today. But if I take Arion, I know that she will fight. Her hand on the knife betrayed her thoughts. I close my eyes, resigning myself to the loss of yet another friend, then step toward Arion.

I take the bridle off his neck. The magic whips and writhes like an angry snake. It wants to stay. I pull slowly, watching the wild magic untangle from Arion's skin. The stones are warm in my hands, warmer than his body heat would account for.

"Quickly, Ayna," Arion urges and the boy steps forward. I turn to him and place the bridle around his neck. Immediately, it clamps onto the boy's skin and settles. The once-turquoise stones turn to jade.

A wide smile breaks across Ayna's face. "Let's go to Faerie."

I laugh, relieved at his eagerness. Not all creatures take well to being Bound. "But first," I say, "to Hammond."

Chapter Eight

Rory

"Penny?" The last voice I want to hear hollers from the hallway. It's Marik, far too close to the kitchen for me to escape undetected. Fear clogs my throat. I can't let him catch me now. He'll give me another dose of *Salvia* and I don't know how long it'll take for me to be this lucid again.

"Quick!" Penny yanks open one of the under counter cabinet doors and frantically waves for me to climb in. It's small, it will be a tight fit, but I scramble into the cramped dark immediately. I expect Penny to close me in and to feel like little more than knees and elbows.

Instead, I bump right into something hard—a door?—which opens and sends me tumbling out onto a bed of soft lilac moss. It's warm under my fingers and smells of honeydew. I roll onto my back and blink at my surroundings. I'm in a room with walls of smooth stone—still in the castle then. Clinging ivy crawls from floor to ceiling. An ornate wood desk rests a few feet in front of me.

I sit up and look behind me. I'm in front of a partially open wooden door. I give it a gentle push and it swings closed.

"I've come out of the closet," I say out loud, a giggle erupting from my mouth. I slap a hand over it and realize that, perhaps, there is still a bit of *Salvia* lingering in my system.

In all my years in Faerie, I've never once questioned how the brownies and other staff could travel through the castle so quickly without being noticed. I wonder how many of these little bolt holes exist. My mind starts to wander and I shake my head roughly.

"Stop it, Rory," I scold myself quietly. "Stay sharp, stay focused." And just to be safe, I dig my thumbnail into a partially healed sore on my wrist. Pain blooms — just like the wild blackberry bramble the Queen had grown under my flesh. For a second, I see it again, the purple canes pushing against my skin from inside, bursting through in a riot of thorns and berries. The pain haunts me again — starting as an itch, then a prickle, then a stinging, biting, *crawling* agony.

I clench my eyes closed and frantically rub my hands over my forearms and up my biceps, reminding myself that it's over, it's gone — besides the slowly healing wounds, there's nothing left of the bramble now.

Unless she left its roots beneath your flesh, a mocking voice that sounds like Marik's whispers to me. *Blackberry brambles grow year after year...*

"Shut up!" I curse the ghostly voice. "You're not real, and she didn't..." I have to believe it. I have to believe that her magic is not *that* strong. Besides, she's a fickle bitch. Her punishments have aways been harsh but fleeting. Out of sight, out of mind, for the most part.

I draw in a steadying breath and am grateful for the chill of the study against my naked skin. It helps to ground me. I shove the memories of thorns pushing at my flesh from the inside into the back of my head and stand.

"Now, where are you?" I murmur, looking around. I'm in an office, but is it the right one? Just because there's a desk, doesn't mean that it belongs to Marik.

Slowly, I spin around. An oaken shield is hanging by the door, but there's no insignia to identify its owner. A humanoid wooden stand rests in the corner beside it. It holds a fur-and-feather cloak, but that's a popular style in Faerie these days. It could belong to any number of people.

The next wall is covered in weapons. I scan them quickly, looking for any that seem familiar. I almost give up hope but then I see it.

There's only one faerie I know who carries a hand-and-a-half sword with a diamond pommel.

"Hurry, Rory," I say as I rock back and forth on my heels. "You're running out of time. There!" I grab the leather quiver and drag it down. I carelessly stick my hand inside, hissing when I stab myself on the spines of a particularly sharp feather in the fletching.

But I find the map.

Grinning, I shove it back in the quiver with the bow and arrows and hook the strap over my shoulder. My gaze lands on the sword. A grin spreads slowly across my face. It would serve him right... I take it off the wall. The baldric is complicated and my fingers are fumbling, but eventually I get it strapped around my waist. The leather bites into my nude skin.

"He doesn't deserve you," I tell it, straightening my spine. "He doesn't deserve either of us."

* * * *

Prince Aries

Ayna is fast—more so than his father, even. And I don't know if it's because his kelpie blood is diluted, but he needs to stop to swim less often. We cover the miles to Hammond in four days.

His sides are heaving, his mouth spewing foam as he shakes his large head. My body feels like melted butter as I slide off his back outside the Djinn and Tonic. The tavern is on the outskirts of town, just before the black asphalt turns to gravel. If not for the hazy lights of downtown in the distance, I'd have thought we were miles from civilization.

My knees threaten to cave and I take a moment, resting my weight against Ayna's flank to stay upright. He knickers a warning and I've barely straightened when he starts to shrink.

"I'm not a leaning post," he says, his voice gritty before he clears his throat. "You owe me a drink."

"I *owe* you nothing," I clarify but pass him a coin. "But I'll treat you to one anyway. We made good time. Better than I expected."

Ayna rests the coin on his thumb and flicks it, then catches it in his palm. He goes to walk inside, and I grab his arm to halt him. "I'm finding Lynilsa and she's opening a portal. Don't wander too far."

"Like I'd miss my chance to leave this hellhole?" Ayna rolls his eyes and heads inside. I take a deep breath of the outside air—it's not fresh by any means, but I know it's going to be better than the liquor-soaked stench of the bar — then step in.

Surprisingly, it smells better than I expected. There is still the bitter tang of alcohol, but my lungs aren't straining. Wood smoke curls out of the stone fireplace and stings my eyes. I blink them clear, then look around the dimly lit bar. Ayna already has a bottle of something dark in his hand. He's sitting near a man in the corner. Vampire, I suspect from the pale, skeletal fingers wrapped around a half-empty glass of something crimson.

There are a few brownies giggling near the banked fireplace and a were-shifter of some kind — I suspect bear, from the breadth of his shoulders — near the stairs.

I spot Lynilsa easily. There aren't too many places a centaur can hide.

She's standing behind the bar, a rag in her hand as she wipes it down. Her lower half is a black and white appaloosa. Her hair is black and hangs loose around her face in the front, but the back follows the length of her spine into a true mane. Except for the bibbed apron, its strings tied at her withers, she's nude. Her breasts are barely covered but like most of her kind, she doesn't seem body shy. I suspect the apron is a nod to food-handling laws and not modesty.

She looks up with a smile as I approach, tucking the cloth into a pocket. "Afternoon, friend. Can I interest you in a glass of the best spring water this side of the Huron?"

I hadn't planned on drinking, but I'm suddenly overwhelmed by the dryness of my throat. Four days of harsh travel with minimal breaks have taken their toll on me. I throw down a scattering of coins. "Yes, and a bowl of tulip bulbs if you have it. Then I'd like to purchase your...*other* services."

"My..." She looks confused but then her brows lift. "Really? Been a long time since a faerie's asked to go home. Are you certain of your choice?" As she speaks, she reaches under the bar and pulls out a wooden bowl, then adds a handful of tulip petals. Her hands are clever as she shreds them into an imitation of a salad.

I frown. "Why would you ask?"

"Seems like there's been a flood of your kind *out* of Faerie lately. I've heard...rumors." Her tail flicks with agitation, the strands whipping into her rump. She turns away, her hindquarters narrowly missing the bar, and grabs a tulip bulb from a wicker basket and a silver shredder. She expertly grates the bulb over the petals, then pushes the bowl to me. She turns again, this time to fill a glass with clear water. She completes her circle until she's facing me again, then plunks it down beside my bowl.

I take a sip to wet my throat. Then, I lower my voice and ask, "What kind of rumors?"

She looks around before biting into her lip. "I despise gossip, I'll have you know, but doesn't seem right letting you go back without warning. Now mind you, I've got no proof of any of this. It's just things I've picked up here and there."

I bite my tongue, restraining my snarky response. I want to say something about that being the very definition of a rumor, but I just nod, urging her to go on. While I listen, I snack on the velvety flower petals. The bulbs are perfectly bitter.

She leans in closer. "They say the land's gone rotten. Trees growing twisted, animals starving for no reason."

I flinch at the thought. Starving? In Faerie? It seems impossible. Faerie has always provided for her children.

"They say the Mirror Lake went cloudy and the May-tree's gone silent."

Icicles stab into my belly and I feel myself go pale.

I've assumed my mother was calling me home for the same petty reasons as always. What if I'm wrong?

What if, by avoiding her missives, I've doomed my homeland and Rory with it? No longer hungry, I abandon my food and stand. "I must return to Faerie immediately."

Lynilsa frowns and pushes my bowl closer toward me. "Sit down. Eat, drink. I can't open the portal without moonlight and even if I could, you'll not make it through the payment process on an empty belly."

Slowly, I sink back down. I pick at the petals but can't stomach the thought of eating one. I've finished half of what she gave me, it will have to be enough. "There isn't another way to speed things up?"

"Afraid not, sweetheart. Besides, you're a faerie. You should know time don't move right between our worlds anyhow. Not much difference between a few minutes or a few hours. You'll get there when you get there."

Chapter Nine

Rory

There's an orgy in the front hall.

I hunker at the top of the staircase and stare down, heart pounding at the expanse of sprawled limbs. A group of fawns are frolicking on a bed of moss to the right of the door. To the left, a spray of naiads lie together in the fountain, sunlight dappling their nude forms.

I find myself overcome with a sense of déjà vu.

I feel like I've been here before. Phantom fingers digging into my skin, teeth biting into me... I lift my hand to my shoulder and shudder as I touch a mouth-shaped wound.

A memory, then, steeped in *Salvia* until it was nearly unrecognizable. Is it better this way, faded like an antique postcard? Or worse, because now I'm left to wonder. Who and how many? Just once, or more?

My body starts to shake and my vision speckles at the edges. I close my eyelids and grind the heels of my hands over them. "Snap out of it, Rory. It's not the first time and if you don't get out of here now, it won't be the *fucking* last either."

A small hand lands on my arm just above my elbow and I flinch away, hands raised to strike before I spot the brownie. I freeze. I cannot convince myself to lay a hand on her, not with her big, teary eyes and quivering lip.

"Penny said Mister Ruari—"

Gods, I hate that name. I don't interrupt her. I just lower my hands, still clenched, to my thighs.

"—was wanting to go outside? Penny said Mr. Ruari needs…" The brownie hesitates, eyes darting to both sides, before she lowers her voice and leans in, "clothing?"

I slowly splay my fingers on my thighs and nod. I've not been excited at the thought of wandering Faerie in the nude but considered the risk worth it if it means getting out.

The brownie looks around again, then pulls a bundle of fabric out of thin air. She shoves it at me. "Here, take it. Don't get caught." She scurries away so quickly I don't have time to thank her.

I dress fast. Of course, they fit perfectly—I wouldn't expect anything else from Penny. The leggings are a soft tan leather that lace up the sides, and the top is a mottled blue-and-green that will blend in well with the forest. If, of course, I make it that far.

I have to get through the orgy first.

I draw in a steadying breath and work to keep my hands from shaking as I re-buckle the sword belt around my waist and replace the quiver over my shoulder.

Then, I descend the stairs.

* * * *

Prince Aries

"So." Ayna plops down at the bar beside me and lifts his empty glass at the waitress, who gets to work pouring him a new one. "Why are we in such a hurry to get back to Faerie now? Seems like you were pretty happy ignoring my dad for plenty of years…"

"Somehow, I don't think your father minded," I say, looking over at him with a lifted brow.

Ayna shrugs. "Beside the point."

I sigh and twist my glass in my hand. "It's complicated."

"Calculus is complicated," Ayna rebuts, his lips twitching like he's trying—and failing—to restrain a smile, "and I figured that out at fourteen. Why don't you give me a chance to decide for myself what's 'too complicated' for me to follow?"

"Have you ever been in a relationship, child?" I ask, twisting in my seat to stare him down. I know he's an adult—legally, by this world's standards anyway—but he's barely more than a twinkle in a faerie's eye.

"Ah. *That* kind of complicated." Ayna accepts his new drink from the bartender but immediately slides the tankard of honeyed liquor to me. "Sounds like you need this more than I do. Boys are complicated."

"What makes you think it's a he?" I ask, but I accept the drink. Just because he's right doesn't mean I need to admit it. Besides, I've never been picky about the gender of my lovers.

Ayna shrugs. "Fifty-fifty shot, so I took it. Was I right?"

I sigh and let go of my stubbornness. If I'm lucky, he'll know soon after we cross over anyway, and it's not like it's a secret. I nod, staring down at the golden liquid for a long moment before I take a drink. "He is. His name is Rory. I knew him from…before."

"Okay…" Ayna draws out the word, clearly hinting for more information.

"He's human," I continue, "or…was? I don't know what he is now."

Ayna frowns. "I see why that could be…complicated?" He doesn't sound sure, though, and I'm not surprised. While interspecies relationships were uncommon, I wouldn't go so far as to call them rare.

I sigh and start over. "He was one of the Borrowed. A changeling," I instantly correct myself, knowing now that the old term was a lie. Borrowed, as if my Queen-mother ever intended on returning them. No, they were stolen. "Brought to Faerie as a babe to be my…I suppose one might call him my soulmate, if faeries had souls."

"Is that…common?" Far from looking disgusted, Ayna only looks intrigued. Part faerie himself, I suppose it's not an unnatural response. Empathy, I've found, is an earned skill and not an innate part of our kind's makeup.

I lift my hand and make a 'so-so' gesture. "It's not *un*common. How much did your father tell you of Faerie?"

Ayna shrugs. "I'd say he told me enough, but perhaps not?"

"For as much as our kind loves sex in all its forms, children are…rare. And those we do have tend to be frail and sickly. My mother lost six blossoms before she birthed me, and they say I was touch-and-go as well, in the beginning. So she sent out the Darrig, her red-skinned hunter, and he returned with a babe. A healthy, human boy with a soul as strong as steel, and she bound him to me. As he breathed, so would I, and as I grew, so would he."

I barely remembered the time before he came. The memories were shrouded in mud and mist. I'd heard the stories from the Darrig himself, of how he stole the babe. At the time, I'd thought the stories amusing — how he'd crept into the village with their round houses and poorly thatched roofs, their wattle-and-daub walls not enough to smother the sound of a crying babe. How the boy's mother had been so drunk with wine, she'd thought the Darrig her husband and lay with him thrice before succumbing to sleep.

The Darrig had laughed at that, knowing he'd left the woman to spawn his half-breed child, and I'd laughed as well.

"Let me guess," Ayna interrupts my musing, "the human resented you for dragging him to Faerie against his will and thought you nothing more than a snobby, spoiled prince. But you, deeply misunderstood, decided to woo him anyway?" Ayna grins, planting his chin in his hand as he leans forward. I feel for a moment like I'm staring into a mirror at my younger self, sitting at the Darrig's knee, but the image quickly fades.

"Quite the opposite, anyway, at least for the first part. I rather suppose he *did* find me a snobby, spoiled prince. That, however, would be because I was quite…entitled in my youth. No, I fear that the resentful one was I."

And how embarrassing a thing to admit out loud.

"I did not enjoy the knowledge that my very existence was only possible because of his…*humanity*. It felt rather like a slap in the face, or…well. Imagine that you were suddenly tied to the life of an ant, an insignificant little insect so far beneath you in the food chain it's literally laughable. Or so I believed at the time. I hate to say that I was quite…rude to him." I cringe as I remember some of my more shameful pranks. "More than rude. I would not blame him for never being able to forgive me."

"Okay, so you pulled his hair a little." Ayna chuckles but the sound fades when he notices that I'm not smiling. "Worse than that, eh?"

"My behavior was unacceptable. I did…terrible things, and let terrible things be done to him. Once, he nearly drowned due to my carelessness." I look away, staring down into my drink again.

"Okay, so…yes. Complicated. And…is he still in Faerie? Is that it?" Ayna asks. As a half-kelpie, and one whose fae half was clearly dominant, I wonder if the thought of drowning even bothers him.

"He was in Old York up until the Blood Storm but…it seems my mother found him. She's using him to call me home," I explain. "Somewhere I promised I would never return." Mostly, I acknowledge to myself, because I'd not wanted to be reminded of Ruari. The pain of losing him had never truly left. I'd just…buried it beneath fresher agonies.

"Your mother…will she hurt him? Is that—oh," He trails off as soon as I flinch.

I bury my face in the tankard and take a long swallow to buy myself a few seconds. "Some people's mothers are warm and kind. The type to…to sing them lullabies and bandage scraped knees. My mother…she's a force of nature."

"Like…an elemental?" Ayna doesn't sound certain.

I smile but there's no humor in it. "Like a hurricane."

I'm well on my way to drunk when Lynilsa finally returns. "As soon as we settle payment, I can get the circle going."

Payment. I wince and stare down at the empty tankards in front of me. Perhaps I should have stopped a few drinks ago but it's too late now. "A memory, right?"

Lynilsa grimaces. "Not just any memory. It needs to be an important one, not just what you ate for breakfast. The spell won't work without sacrifice."

"Of course…" I sigh. "Do I choose, or…?"

"The spell chooses. I'm sorry." Worse, she did *look* apologetic. As if she would do it a different way if she had a choice.

I push away from the table and stand. Waiting won't change the outcome, so we might as well get on with it. "Lead the way."

Ayna and I follow her through the tavern and out of the back door into a garden. It's nice enough. Nothing will ever compare to the beauty of my homeland but there are some places in this world, like this, that are almost right. Places that smell the same, even if they don't feel it. I run my fingers along a snaking vine, smiling as the leaves tilt toward me in greeting.

"Will just take a moment," Lynilsa says, picking her way carefully through the wild tangle of plants. Her hooves click when she steps out onto a cobblestone square at the garden's heart.

I stop at the edge. Ayna stands at my side, and together we watch as she walks over to a pole near the other side, pulling a mirror from her pocket. It takes her only a moment to hang it, then a second more to adjust it to her liking. A circle of moonlight reflects off it onto the stones. "Kneel at the center of the circle please," she says, her voice calm and quiet.

I obey but look to Ayna. "You can still change your mind and stay."

"No way." He hurries over, like if he waits I'll leave without him, and kneels beside me. "I've been dreaming of this since my first shift. Soon as I realized I'd never be normal here." He smiles but I can tell the words hurt more than he wanted to let on.

I pat his shoulder but don't speak. There's nothing I can say to make it better for him and sometimes saying nothing is the best choice. He seems to understand.

Turning back to Lynilsa, I clear the lump from my throat and ask, "Where will the portal open? In Faerie, I mean?"

"There's no way to know for certain. Just that it will open where you are meant to be." She pauses, looking between Ayna and me. "He is Bound to you, yes?"

"He is," I agree.

"Good. You should arrive together then." The thought that we wouldn't hadn't even crossed my mind but I suppose it should have. Maybe if I hadn't downed half a gallon of liquor, it would have. Two faeries means two fates. Her words allayed a worry I didn't know I should have.

Lynilsa pulls a small flute from her pocket. "When I start to play, the spell will begin. Do not move. Do not leave the circle. Once I've begun, you cannot change your mind."

"I understand," I agree. Ayna echoes me.

Lynilsa waits a moment, as if to give us a second to change our mind, then lifts the flute. Just before she begins, she says, "Safe travels. May Faerie welcome you and you find comfort in her arms."

Then, she starts to play.

Chapter Ten

Rory

I'm free of the castle.

Not quite unmolested, but I'm alive and in one piece and that alone is more than I ever imagined I'd achieve. Now to stay that way. How long before Marik realizes that he can't find me because I'm not there? How long until he sends guards — or worse, himself — outside the castle walls?

I shudder and am grateful when I finally sink into the safety of the shadows at the forest's edge. Safety, at least, from potential prying eyes. I suddenly wonder, though, how safe I really am.

There's something dark in the forest — I feel it in the air, an oppressive weight, an unseen danger.

"You're crazy," I say out loud but flinch at the way my voice seems to echo against the trees. I press my lips together and hold my breath but nothing leaps out to attack me.

I've been in these woods more times than I can count. They've never seemed this...awake. Awake, and angry. I shiver but force myself forward. The ground is cold beneath my bare feet. I'm grateful for the clothing but I wish the brownie had brought me boots.

Not that I can blame her for not thinking about it, especially since I hadn't thought to ask. The faeries don't wear them. Their soles are tough as stone and their steps light enough many could literally walk across water.

I snicker at the thought. What would those crazy humans say, those religious nutjobs and zealots, if they could see it? Would they think the faerie their messiah, or a demon sent to steal their soul?

Of course, since demons had been revealed to be real, living breathing creatures, most humans had started reevaluating their thoughts of the afterlife. Or at least, they'd certainly been more careful about what they said out loud. I wonder sometimes what it had been like before the Elyries had been dragged into the open.

I grew up knowing that I, as a human, was far weaker than any of the creatures that fill this world. Even the smallest of wild animals could kill me easily if it chose. Nothing here is benign. I can't even imagine growing up in a world where I was — or even *thought* I was — at the top of the food chain.

No wonder the Blanks had been so virulently angry.

It's harder to walk through the forest paths than I remember. My feet used to be tough as leather but it seems my time on Earth had softened them, an irony I can't quite get past. My hands had toughened and cracked from the bitter cold winters, and my skin had chapped from the pollution, but my feet? They'd grown soft and weak. Shoes…shoes were a blessing I'd kill to have now.

I try to stick to the moss where I can, but it's not possible to avoid the sharp rocks and twigs completely. I refuse to be caught and dragged back to that hellhole over something as stupid as a bit of pain though, so I keep walking.

To distract myself, I look around for anything familiar. I don't spot anything I recognize. What I do see is…alarming. Trees that should be tall and proud are stooped and limp. What was once probably a small stream looks like an oil spill creeping along the roots system.

I shiver and walk faster. The air grows colder and shadows stretch toward me like grasping fingers. *Is this real, this oppressive weight on the air, this tremor-terror? Or is this another symptom of my patchwork lucidity?*

I almost convince myself that it's the *Salvia*.

Then, I see a meadow. For the first time since entering the forest, I feel peace. Golden sunlight bathes a bed of freckle-nose tulips. Their velvet cream petals, blushed and bespeckled, have always been my favorite. Larger than their earthly cousins, they sway gently from side to side in the still, windless air.

I step into the silent meadow, eager to scent their sweet fragrance for the first time in ages. Instead, all I smell is rot. I freeze two steps from the nearest flower and look around for the source. I see no carcass, no bloated bodies to blame it on, and frown. I shake my head and go to kneel but before I can, a ladybird sings nearby. The blue feathered fowl, similar in size to a quail but with wings like a hummingbird, flies quickly into the meadow, chirping happily as she heads straight for a tulip near the center of the flowerbed. She hovers near the fist sized bulb, lowering her bill to the petals to gather the sweet nectar.

But suddenly, the flowers open like mouths. Sharp, thorny green protrusions like teeth snap at the air. The bird startles upward but one of the tulips is faster. It snaps its jaws — *can a flower* have *jaws?* — around the body of the bird and crushes it.

The ladybird screams and I start to gag at the violent sight, falling back onto my ass and scuttling backward, away from the monstrous flowers. The other tulips are now violent mouths, straining toward the explosion of feathers and blood like starving things.

I watch, horrified, as the killer plants strip the poor bird to bones and swallow those too before they settle, looking again like nothing more than pretty flowers.

I shudder and stand, backing away from the serene meadow and back into the safety — though now I worry what other horrors await me in the shadows — of the forest.

* * * *

Aries

I fall to my knees on familiar lavender moss and almost burst into tears. I didn't realize how much I'd missed Faerie — didn't think I'd missed her at all — until I'd come back. Her air wraps around me, warm and soft, like a lover's embrace. There's an edge to it, though, an anger.

Faerie might have accepted me back, her prodigal son, but she's not happy with me. My absence, I realize, has been noted. I press my palm to the soft ground and whisper an apology.

Her forgiveness is quick to come.

As the wind settles, I scour my memory for what was taken but can find nothing obvious gone. No large blanks, no gaping holes. Whatever it was, I do not miss it.

"Dude! The grass is *purple*?" Ayna blurts beside me, his voice loud and startling.

"I thought you said that Arion told you about Faerie?" I answer dryly.

"Well...like about the different Courts and the Queen and all that, but he never said nothing about purple grass or...or...trees with eyes. Why is that one staring at me?"

I turn to look at Ayna, then follow his gaze to a large willow that is, indeed, staring at him. I smile and close my eyes, listening. "She wants to know why the young one is so loud."

"The young...I'm an adult, you know!" Ayna, adult or not, pouts as he says it.

I chuckle. "In Faerie, adulthood is measured by wisdom and courage, not years of life. She says you are barely more than a sprout. She says she will speak to you when you can tell her the number of leaves on the Celiath Tree." I try to hold back my smirk but nod at the Willow.

The Celiath Tree is an interesting one. I'd fallen for the riddle myself once. I'd spent weeks upon weeks counting leaves but the number always changed. The Celiath Tree is in constant flux, growing and shrinking and twisting without warning. I'd gotten so frustrated I'd thought of burning it down — then, I'd reasoned, the answer would be *none*.

Thankfully, I'd overcome my irrational anger before succumbing to such a vile act. It had still taken me ages before I thought to just *ask* the tree how many leaves she held.

I wonder how long it will take Ayna.

Ayna laughs. "Why would I want to speak to a tree anyway?"

I cringe and step away from the willow, who has already started to bristle. Her branches whip wildly as her anger starts to gather like a growing storm and the air seems to grow icy.

Ayna, thankfully, is not fully without sense. He lifts his hands placatingly and gives a little bow. "My apologies, I meant no offense. I am newly arrived and clearly have much to learn." If his words came out strangled by his pride, at least the willow chose not to take further offense. Slowly, her branches still, though the air remains frigid.

"Come, Ayna. It is perhaps best we take our leave."

"I think you may be right," Ayna agrees, and together we step onto the narrow, winding path leading further into the forest. "How do you know which direction to go?"

"We don't," I answer honestly. "But Faerie brought us here for a reason and she would not allow us to be steered wrong." I say the words with confidence, though inwardly I have my doubts. Something feels very wrong in the woods around me.

Chapter Eleven

Rory

Night threatens as the shadows grow long around me. I glance up at the canopy above me, wondering how much moonlight will make it through. Will it be too dark for me to see? Can I risk stumbling around in these woods so clearly full of wrong, twisted things?

But can I risk resting? Have they realized I've left the castle yet? Are they already giving chase?

A shudder creeps down my spine at the thought of being hunted again. The memories of the hounds' needle-sharp teeth in my flesh, this time with no laughing faerie prince to call them off.

My fear begs me to keep moving and I almost do, until my inner monster starts to stir. *"Wait…listen."*

Reluctantly, I obey.

Time seems to stretch as I close my eyes and cock my head, straining to hear whatever caught his attention. For several moments, I hear nothing but then, just as I'm about to give up, I hear it. Whispers from the shadows.

"Run, run, run fast, run far, they chase with teeth and claws. Run, run, run quick, don't stall, we'll break you with our jaws." The words are not spoken aloud. Instead, my monster *feels* them. He tastes their intentions, sharp as salt.

Immediately, I hunker down to a crouch, perched on my toes. I dig my fingers into the cold, damp dirt. Something in the shadows wants me afraid. Something in the shadows wants me to flee. So they can give chase?

I strain my senses and slowly, I feel it. This tiny clearing, ringed by evergreens, is sheltered from the hungry beasts so long as the moon watches from the sky. If I am going to rest, here is the safest place.

It is a risk I hate taking. I may be safe from whatever beasts are stalking the shadows, but this sacred circle will not protect me from the chasing fae. Still, there's no certainty yet that I'm being pursued, and there is definitely something out there now wanting to eat the flesh from my bones.

Slowly I sink down onto my butt. The ground is cold and I start to shiver. Curling on my side does little to conserve warmth, and it takes a long time for me to fall asleep.

I feel like I've barely closed my eyes when something startles me awake. A twig breaking? I sit up and stare between the trees. The shadows are longer, predawn stretching them out like fingers.

Is it an animal, or have I run out of time?

I try to stand but a creeping vine I hadn't seen snags my ankle, dragging me back to the ground. My mouth opens on a yelp but before the sound escapes, a leaf snakes into my mouth. I struggle to get free but a tree root clamps down on my back, holding me still.

The weight makes it hard to breathe. Panic grows like speleothems in my chest. Sharp, it stabs at me from the inside and I find it hard to stay grounded in this moment when my mind is flashing back to the Queen's tortures.

I cannot let myself go back there.

My terror grows bitter and strong. The monster in my ribcage starts to wake just as I hear the voices.

Faeries.

And they are coming my way.

* * * *

Prince Aries

"So, this is where you met my father?" Ayna asks, his voice loud in the otherwise silent forest as he lopes along beside me. He makes little effort to avoid stomping with his hooves and I wince every time he breaks a twig or snaps the stem of a plant. Not because I particularly care for them — Faerie is hardy and they will grow back quickly — but because the sound echoes and multiplies.

"It's not what I expected," Ayna continues and I rub my eyes, exasperated. Twice now, I've asked him to speak softer. He obliges for a few moments but too soon, his voice rises again. "I mean, the colors are weird, but...the trees still look like trees."

"Did you expect them to look like cows?" I ask dryly, and crouch down to examine the path. Is that a footprint? I trace the soft curve of what might be a heel. If it's Rory, we are going in the right direction. If it's not...well, I guess we'll find out.

"No? I don't know. I expected something...more. Like...whimsy or something. More than just eyes, anyway. Figured I'd feel like Alix in Wanderland."

I snort and stand back up. "Wanderland was somebody's acid trip. Faerie is real."

"Wanderland is a treasured piece of American literature!"

"Wanderland is a poor rip off of a book by Lewis Carroll," I reply absently, staring at the path. There's something…odd ahead.

"Who's Lewis Carroll?" Ayna asks. Whatever I'm seeing, he doesn't seem to notice.

"A man well before your time," I admit, "and an excellent author of literary nonsense. Now hush. There's something here."

"Is it him? Your human?"

"Hush," I say again, a quiet hiss.

Thankfully, he goes silent.

I walk ahead of him, ears peeled and eyes searching. I spot the evergreens first. They are leaning forward, a circle half-bent, as if staring at something below them. I loosen my sword in her sheath as I get closer. It could be Rory, but it could also be a daeva or a borrig or any number of carnivorous creatures excited to taste faerie blood.

The trees seem to sigh as I approach, limbs sagging. They reek of fear—syrup gone rancid. I draw my blade fully as I go on high alert and hold up my left hand toward Ayna. *Stay*, I silently order, hoping he understands. More than that, hoping he listens.

Ayna might only be half-kelpie but he's inherited all of their typical wildness. I trust that he will not put himself or me in harm's way intentionally, but I do not trust that he won't wander away at the first sight of a will-o'-the-wisp. At least he won't drown in whatever body of water they lead him to.

Putting my worries from my mind, I step inside the evergreen circle.

At the very heart is a mound made of overturned dirt, twining vines and tangled roots. They are writhing like a nest of snakes, the leaves above me shaking like a warning rattle.

The trees are frightened into wordless terror by whatever creature they've caught and are attempting to bury. As soon as I realize that, I notice that the erratic movement of the roots is not an intentional decision on the trees part — it's a reaction to the violence occurring just below the surface.

The dirt churns. With an explosion of gravel and dust, a hand forces its way through the netted roots. The fingers are slender and pale as bone, tipped with long, wickedly sharp obsidian claws. They curve like a raptor's. The creature's wrist is skeletal as it emerges, but humanoid. Dirt clings to the chalky flesh in streaks.

I grip the hilt of my sword and merge into the nearest shadow, breathing deeply to quiet my heartbeat. Whatever beast this is — a riot of burning coal hair appears — I don't know how strong their senses are.

Eyes of emerald fire glare at me as the creature drags itself free. Dirt clings in clumps to long, feathery eyelashes and leaves its skin stained and mottled. Whatever monster this is, I've never seen one of its kind before. There's something feline about its face — perhaps the shape of its nose — but its teeth are silver and needle-sharp.

I stumble back a step in shock. It's humanoid in shape but there's nothing human about it, and while I sense Faerie magic, it seems to ebb and flow like a tide. Some other, darker wixcraft churns beneath it.

Was it once a faerie, now corrupted by whatever strange magic has polluted this world? It wears a faerie bow on its back, the white wood gleaming. At its hip rests a sword but it doesn't seem to notice it. That, or it knows its claws are deadlier weapons. Something dark and oily seems to coat their sharp length. Venom, I wonder?

It lets loose a loud, threatening growl. I plant my feet and start to lift my blade. It moves more quickly than a creature its size should. Before I'm ready, it lunges.

Chapter Twelve

Prince Aries

I slip to the side just in time to narrowly avoid being tackled, but I'm not quick enough to avoid the claws. They are razor sharp as they slash through the fabric of my shirt and catch in my cloak, nearly choking me as it pulls. The creature hisses. I release the clasp at my throat and let the cloak slide free. The sudden release of pressure makes the monster stumble and I take the opportunity for a quick jab.

It's fast, back bowing enough that the sharp edge of the blade only opens a line of fire across its belly. Ink-thick violet blood seeps from the shallow wound. The creature yowls and I take the moment to turn, backing further into the grove while maintaining its line of sight.

I want to keep its attention on me, not Ayna who's lurking just a few feet away — far nearer than I'd like him to be, unarmed and untested in battle as he is. The creature stalks closer to me, ignoring Ayna as I hoped.

It walks, stooped forward, with bent knees, claws at the ready.

It steps into the sunlight and its hair seems to catch fire, skin nearly translucent. The monster curls its lips back and growls, but I freeze, lowering my sword in shock again.

Now, here in the sunlight, I recognize him. It's the eyes, the bottle-green flames burning into my soul.

"Ruari?"

He lunges again but this time, I'm too slow to dodge. He slams into me and together, we fall back into the dirt.

Rory

"*Ruari?*"

The old name comes to me as if through water — *deep water, cold water, swirling-down-the drain-water* — and I struggle against the sound. I am tired and here — *where is here?* — is calm and quiet. But that name, spoken in that voice, it hooks me deep in my chest and tugs, dragging me back to the surface, where I waken with a gasp.

Except I wasn't asleep, I realize, eyes blinking down at a frightened faerie. Aries, his dark skin ashy. Someone's bone-white hand tipped with hooked black claws is digging into his chest, each nail drawing beads of blue blood.

My hand, I realize, just in time for the agonizing pain to strike me. I fall to the side in the grave-shallow pit, curling into fetal position, with a cry as my body starts to shake, bones rearranging. My monster's claws shrink, reabsorbed like acid beneath my skin, leaving behind only a bitter burning. My jaw aches as my teeth start to fall out, poking my gums and tongue as I spit them, along with large globs of blood-streaked saliva, onto the ground. I gag at the feeling of them passing my lips, already starting to soften like worms. Within seconds, they are little more than slime in the mud. I stare at them, disgusted but unable – or unwilling – to stare at Aries instead.

Aries, Prince of Faerie, whose blood I've fed to this cold, bitter ground. I can feel it stirring, thirsting. Aries, who was left behind on Earth when the Queen had her minions drag me through the portal here. Had he followed me, or did he stumble upon me by chance?

Will he aid me in my escape or prove to be my downfall?

"Ruari?" Aries says again, his voice holding that same shock that pulled me back from wherever I go when the monster wakes.

"Rory," I correct him, my voice snapping and sharp. "It's Rory."

"Rory," he says softer. "What – "

"I don't know," I interrupt him, clenching my fists and forcing myself to my feet, still unwilling to meet his gaze. "I did a spell and it went a bit sideways. I don't want to talk about it."

Rather, I don't know enough to speak of it with any intelligence – at this point, Aries has seen more of my monster than I have. I drag myself out of the hole we'd somehow ended up in – I don't recall it being here when I fell asleep – and into the sunlight. It's bright and stings my eyes. Aries is more graceful as he follows me. I raise my hand to shield them just in time to see movement in the trees.

It is the faeries coming to steal me again, to drag me back to the castle. What will the Queen do to me this time? Now that Aries is here as she wished, will she kill me? Or, worse—will she keep me alive, her own personal torture slave for the rest of eternity?

I feel my monster stirring again, weakly now, but I know it won't stay this way. I go to step back, to turn and run—any direction, anywhere I can—but my heel hits only air. Before I can fall, Aries is there, holding me up.

"Let me go, let me *go*." I try to squirm free, but Aries holds me tighter.

"Calm down, Rory, what are you—?" His gaze tracks mine, landing on the figure in the woods. "That's Ayna. He's with me."

I go still, not certain if that's better or not. "And is he—are *you*—here to take me back?"

"To the castle?" Aries asks, and he sounds confused. But I do not know if I can trust how he sounds, not when he lies so well without even having to speak. I trusted him once before and look where it got me. Dragged from an empty bed and turned into a faerie plaything.

"I won't go," I say, resolute. My determination turns my voice to iron.

"Then where are we headed?" Aries asks and I jerk, surprised that he doesn't argue. Should I answer? Is he tricking me again?

Can I trust him?

I don't know.

"Unless we stumble upon a tear, Earth is out of the question," I say in place of an answer.

"You're right. A Tear is a possibility," Aries acknowledges, "but not one I'd like to bank on."

"Agreed." Tears are random and rare. The odds of stumbling on one now when I need one are astronomical. I meet his gaze and try to gauge his thoughts. I've never been able to read him well enough to know his mind.

"Why are you here, Aries?" I finally break down and ask the question haunting my mind.

He lifts his brows, surprise coloring his expression. *Is it real or feigned*? "For you," he answers.

He must believe it's true to speak it aloud.

"Are you—either of you," I add, thinking of the faerie in the woods, "working on your mother's orders?" I clarify. Will he answer the question or artfully dodge?

"Neither I nor Ayna are working on my mother's orders, or the orders of any of her people," he says clearly and slowly. His words ring with truth. "My mother sent me a letter with *this* – " He shoves his hand in his pocket and pulls out a cloth handkerchief. He lets it unfold, revealing a taped up envelope. He hands it to me and I tear it open. Inside is my necklace. I lift my hand to my neck, where the pendant used to hang until the Queen ordered it removed from my neck.

At least the bastard faerie's hand had blistered in the process. I hope it hurt.

I pull it free, letting the envelope fall as I prepare for him to yank the jewelry away at the last second. He doesn't. I bring the ends of the chain together and hook the latch with shaking hands. Immediately, my shoulders sag. It is heavy, but a weight I am grateful to bear.

Iron is my best defense in this world.

"I knew she had you, so I came. I did not expect to find you this quickly, already freed." Aries gives me a smile. It's small, a gift just for me. I still don't trust him.

"Will you go to her?" I ask.

"I would find her and make her pay for whatever crimes she's committed against you," Aries says, his voice dark, "if that's what you wish."

"She would string you up for the crows," I scoff. "You are no match for her."

"But I would do it still, if you asked. I am not here on her orders, and I will not turn you over to her hand, Rory. I came only to secure your freedom in whatever way was necessary." Aries cannot lie, no faerie can, so I know I must believe him, but it's hard.

Why did he come for me now but leave me then? What must he want me for? I glance toward the stranger in the woods and know I will not ask him. Not here, anyway, and not now.

"I am going to the Unsidhe," I blurt, steeling my shoulders to brace for his reaction.

Again he surprises me. He shows no anger, just surprise that turns quickly to acceptance. "I do not know the way, but I would see you safely to the border."

"But not beyond?" I ask, feeling an unexpected and unwarranted hurt. He owes me nothing, not even the escort.

"They would not welcome my presence."

"But you think they'll welcome mine?" I clarify and cross my arms protectively across my chest. The air seems to grow chillier as we speak and I shiver.

"I believe they'll find you interesting. And I think that King Adalberon would find a certain amusement in providing sanctuary to someone fleeing the Queen's court." Aries frowns and looks around. "We should move. The air grows cold. There is something not right nearby."

I think to tell him of the bed of unnaturally hungry flowers but he's already moving, waving the stranger — Ayna — to follow. He steps out of the shadows. He is taller than me — no surprise, many men are — but looks younger. I feel that he is older than he appears, though. His hair is as curly as mine, but darker. It falls much longer as well.

He stares at me warily and I stare back, not bothering to hide my curiosity. I don't ask any of the million questions twirling through my head. Aries is already walking, striding into the shadows with determination in his steps. Besides, it's none of my business if Aries has taken another lover. I have no claim on him now — I never did.

Chapter Thirteen

Prince Aries

Ayna is mercifully quiet as we walk. I think he's intimidated by Rory. I can't blame him. Every time I look back to make sure I haven't lost them, Rory's eyes are on Ayna. Sometimes narrowed, sometimes sharp, sometimes curious — but always on Ayna. Something like jealousy twists in my stomach.

"Ayna," I snap, and his attention jerks to me. "Come and look at this."

It's just a gild'a lily but I spend several long moments crouched beside it with the boy, explaining which parts of the golden plant are safe to eat and which have medicinal properties — the roots give a burst of energy, like being hooked up to a caffeine drip with an equally impressive crash at the end, the petals will heal almost any wound. The pollen gives a nice, gentle flavoring to a tea.

Ayna listens, rapt. Behind him, Rory is glaring. I smirk and run my fingers over the long yellow stigma. The bulb seems to shudder and Rory huffs. "We need to move. If you're going to sexually assault a flower, I'll move forward on my own."

"Jealous, sweetheart?" I tease.

Rory growls—an animalistic sound that lifts the hair on the back of my neck and shifts my weight to my toes, preparing me to run. I clamp down on the instinctive fear and plant my feet.

"If we get caught here, you'll be heralded back at the castle as a hero. The prodigal prince returned. I'll be a *Salvia* Slut. So excuse me if I'm not all that interested in a botany lesson," Rory hisses between sharply clenched teeth.

I flinch hard at the reference to *Salvia*, barely hearing anything after the word. A disgusting flower that turns sentient beings into little more than sexed-up plants. I wipe my palms on my thighs and stand, body cold. "That's not something to joke of, Rory. There's nothing amusing in what that wretched herb does to people."

I wonder where he's even heard of it. I wrack my memory but as far as I'm aware, the herb had fallen out of favor with the court. I'd met only a scant handful of the Sluts. They were mewling, messy things, overcome with indiscriminate need for the next cunt or cock. I'd played with one once but found no joy in the encounter. It was like fucking a doll. To my knowledge, until Ruari, it was the only time my magic hadn't ended in my lover's death.

It was a testament to the strength of the *Salvia* that not even a Leanan Sidhe could inspire a Slut to perform beyond sex games.

Rory's face turns red — with shame or anger, I wonder? — and he clenches his fists until the knuckles turn white. *Anger,* I decide. Has he seen someone on *Salvia?* Perhaps it's come back into favor at my mother's court.

"Whatever," he finally huffs, pushing past me as he continues walking. His shoulder rams into mine hard enough that I stumble. "We need to get moving."

"He's a feisty one," Ayna mutters, staring at Rory's back.

"That he is. He's also probably right. We should go." I hate admitting when I'm wrong but I'm better at it now then I used to be, even if it still grates. Ayna stays in step with me and now, with Rory just ahead of us, he's quiet.

The suns are high in the sky when Rory comes to an abrupt stop. In two steps, I'm at his side, staring at a meadow of gently swaying, freckle-nosed tulips. I see nothing that should have prompted the sudden halt.

"Rory —" I start to ask, but he grabs my arm in a tight grip and shushes me. Slowly, he crouches, fingers skimming over the dirt until he grabs a flat stone. *A good one for skipping,* I think, just as he throws it, wrist twisting, toward the bed of flowers.

As soon as it skims past the first row, the flowers come to life, petals opening to reveal sharp teeth and the stench of rot. Behind me, Ayna curses. "What the fuck are *those?*"

"Something not natural," I respond absently, staring in horror at the carnivorous plants. I want to step closer, to examine the plants for the cause of the grotesque mutation, but an equally large part of me wants to turn and run in the other direction. "What is wrong with Faerie?" I murmur.

"What *isn't*?" Rory answers snidely. "Let's circle around."

"Into the *woods*? What if the fucking *trees* try to eat us now?" Ayna whines, his voice high and scared.

I plan to say something comforting but Rory beats me to it. "We've been in the woods all day, dumbass. If there are flesh-eating trees, then we're in the same position we were an hour ago."

"Yeah, but an hour ago I didn't realize that was a possibility!" Ayna yelps.

Rory rolls his eyes and I can't help but smirk. This is not the same gentle, soft-spoken boy I'd teased for years. That boy wouldn't have bitten back. "You can choose to stay here, alone, with the definitely murderous flowers, or come with us into the maybe murderous trees. Your choice."

"Hell of a choice," Ayna mutters. He pins me with a sullen glare. "This is not what I expected Faerie to be like."

"Your father warned you that this wasn't going to be a fairy tale," I point out, then start to follow Rory along the edge of the glade, out of the reach of the tulips.

"No one mentioned it was going to be a horror story instead," Ayna grumbles, but he follows nonetheless — practically walking on my heels to keep close. In many ways, he's like a puppy, eager and skittish.

Rory, though, is a Pit Bull. The lens I've been viewing him through — of young Ruari, with his dewy eyes and quivering jaw, is starting to blur and crack. I grin, already anticipating the snappy, biting words he'll fling at me in the morning if he wakes with elfknots.

Perhaps on the run from my mother's Court is not the best time for pranks, but I want to tease him one last time before I hand him over to the Unsidhe and their land of winter and cold. I want to taste the heat of his anger — cinnamon sharp.

We enter the shadowy woods again.

* * * *

Rory

As the second sun dips below the tree line and the shadows begin to lengthen, our progress starts to slow. My night vision has improved drastically since the magical change I underwent, the colors fading out to shades of black and gray, but Ayna is stumbling. The third time he trips, I sigh and Aries slows even further.

"We should find a place to camp soon," Aries says, sounding as reluctant as I feel.

As much as I want to keep walking, my feet are aching. Besides, I know that however dangerous the woods may be during the day, they'll be doubly so now. We continue moving until we come upon a henge of moss-kissed stones.

Without speaking, we all stop. There's a calmness to the air here. While the rest of the forest has felt humid and muggy, here is cool. There's a faint breeze, just enough to stir my curls, and it smells of the sea. Just beyond the farthest standing stone, the still waters of an oxbow lake glistens in the starlight.

"I have no memory of this place..." Aries muses, breaking the silence as we stare at the stones.

"That may be...but it's not new." I reach out and tough the well-worn surface of the nearest. It's smooth in the way only something exposed to the elements for many years can be, with thick vines creeping over the surface. They feel old.

"I don't like it," Ayna grumbles, arms crossed over his chest and jaw set. "If you don't remember it, we should find somewhere else."

I laugh and the sound comes out cold. "Our dear Aries here ran away from Faerie so long ago, I'm surprised he remembers anything. I certainly don't plan on leaving the first place that's felt safe based off his *memory*."

Whether he remembers it or not, there's something…familiar. It reminds me of the lake I used to swim in. I step into the center of the henge and stare. It *could* be the same, I suppose…the shape is right, though there'd only been trees along this bank back then. Now, the forest encircles the U-shaped water.

"Those flowers felt safe too, until they tried to *eat* us," Ayna whines.

"If they'd tried to eat you, you'd be bleeding," I reply, voice dry. "Go somewhere else if you'd like, but I'm staying here." I start scanning the ground for a dry — or semi-dry — place to settle.

"Aries…" Ayna pleads, but Aries steps into the circle as well.

"Hush," is his answer. "Rory's right. Here is as good a place as anywhere. Too much of the forest has changed to be certain of safety anywhere. Here, Rory," Aries says.

I turn toward him. He's holding out a bundle of fabric — a bedroll, I realize, and I flush. "I don't need your pity," I snap, crossing my arms to hide my clenched fists. *Do I want to sleep where he's slept?*

"It's not pity. I've got one for each of us. Don't let your stubbornness tonight slow us down tomorrow." He holds it out until I take it. It's soft and thick, warmer even than the cloak I'd stolen. When I unroll it, even the ground seems to sigh. I don't slide in right away. Instead, I sit on it and pull my knees up, arms draped loosely atop them.

"I don't suppose you have any food in there? I'm starving," Ayna asks as he takes his bedroll from Aries.

"I've got a bit, but we'll have to ration it. Faerie won't let us starve —"

Probably, I think, but don't interrupt out loud. The Faerie we walk in now is not the one of my memories. She feels weary.

Aries keeps speaking, "I suspect our journey won't be easy." He hands over an airtight packet of dried meat to Ayna, then chucks one at me. It lands in my lap.

I tear it open with my teeth, already salivating. Just because I might not starve to death here doesn't mean that my stomach isn't aching with hunger. And beneath that ache is another, a twisting, cramping pain from the withdrawals. How long until they disappear completely? It seems to be fading more quickly this time around — is that because of the strange magic under my skin, or because I wasn't kept dosed as long?

I don't know, and I don't know if it even matters. I won't allow myself to be dosed again. This time, I have a sword at my side. I'll fall on it before I let Marik or his minions drag me back to the Queen's bed.

I wait until Aries leaves to scout the perimeter of the henge, melting into the shadows like a ghost, before I turn to Ayna. I roll up onto the balls of my feet and crouch. Ayna looks at me with wary eyes, but not wary enough. He's too naïve for this place, this land that makes murderers out of martyrs and jades even the sweetest of youth.

"You shouldn't have come," I say, my voice sharp in the cooling twilight air. "Aries may claim your safety but even a man who cannot lie does not necessarily speak the truth." Not in its entirety, at least. Faeries have long perfected the art of twisting words.

"He promised me nothing but a path to Faerie, which he has done," Ayna says, and he sets his jaw. Unlike me, he stays standing, shoulders back.

I stare at him for a long moment. There's something about the stubborn tilt of his head...I let my gaze follow his body down to the shiny black hooves. "You're a kelpie... One of Arion's get?" It's a guess but from the way he flinches, a good one.

"I am his second son," Ayna answers, pride staining his voice.

"And your mother a human..." I muse, still staring at the hooves. He must be a half-breed. No kelpie I'd ever met—and I'd met several—would choose a half-form if they had a choice to glamour it. What prey would be stupid enough to follow a kelpie into deep waters?

I see Ayna's hands clench and when I look back at his face, his cheeks are red with anger. "You gotta problem with that?"

"No problem," I answer, and it's true. "I just never thought I'd see the day where Arion, the Sterling Scourge, would bed a mortal. He generally preferred to drown them."

Twice, he'd dragged me into roiling rivers and laughed as I sputtered. I can still taste the river water burning at the back of my throat if I close my eyes.

"My mother was never stupid enough to swim with him," Ayna answers.

It's telling that he doesn't defend his father. There were no false claims that "My father would *never*." Instead, he praises his mother…perhaps Arion had not changed as much as I imagined. Perhaps his mother is one of those rare, steel-spined women.

Perhaps the boy is not as naïve as I feared.

"You should not have let him bring you to Faerie." I curl my toes in the dirt. It is cold and moist.

"I didn't 'let' him do anything. I asked to come. I *chose* to come," Ayna answers, and I hear the truth in his words.

"This is not a nice place." I lower my eyes to a lonely weed. I reach out a finger and stroke the stem — the plant hisses. "It will break you, and then take the pieces that remain and mold you into something else…something sharp."

I look at my hands — normal hands with normal fingers, but beneath them, I know there are dagger claws. "Something you won't like."

"Maybe Faerie broke *you*," Ayna says, voice sullen, his words hitting me like a mallet strike, "but it won't me."

I sigh. He has not felt her yet, not heard her whispers, her cries, not tasted her bitter pain. I know, because he still calls her 'it'. My warnings will only fall on deaf ears. He will have to learn the hard way.

I drop it. I mean to sink back on my butt and ignore him but the next words slip out on their own. "You cannot have Aries."

The words scatter heavy like coins. I didn't mean to speak them. They've betrayed me. I want to not care about the Prince or his consorts. Let him fuck the world and everyone in it, as long as he leaves me alone...but I can't.

He is *mine,* hate him though I might.

"You *cannot* have him," I repeat, but this time, it is a plea. Not a bargain, I am not yet that desperate. I don't want him, don't *want* to want him...but I don't want anyone else to have him, either.

Ayna looks uncomfortable. "Um...you're looking a bit...vampy, man."

I feel it now, the fullness of my mouth. I jerk my hand up and feel the sharp teeth. It's a struggle to tuck them away.

"Look," Ayna continues, "I don't want Aries. I'm too young to settle down and even if I wanted to, you and him have some fucked-up past relationship drama to work through. I'm not touching that mess with a ten-foot pole...or a seven-inch one, if you know what I mean..." He suddenly grins and the innuendo startles a laugh out of me. I relax, finally sinking back on to my sleeping bag.

"Okay...okay." I repeat it to myself, as I tuck the possessiveness back down. I hear the rustle of a cloak coming from behind the henge and stiffen. I move my hand to the hilt of the sword at my waist but it's just Aries. He steps out of the woods with a frown, staring between me and Ayna.

After a second, he seems to relax. I wonder what he expected, a catfight? "I've hidden our tracks as best I can," he says, "and asked Faerie to lay a false one leading away from here. We should be safe until first dawn, at least."

"Faerie is as like to lead them to us as away, regardless what you asked," I snap back. "Someone should keep watch." I slide into my sleeping bag and glare at Aries, anger burning my chest. It is an old anger. I'd never dealt with his abandonment or the horrors he'd left me to all those years ago…I'd escaped to Earth and bound the emotions in magic murals rather than deal with them. "You can go first."

I close my eyes and resolutely try to fall asleep. He laughs, the sound soft, and I try not to let it affect me. Now that I'm lying down, though, my exhaustion seems to have fled. All I can think of is Aries nearby. There's so much I want to ask him…so much I want to say.

Why did you leave me?
Did you ever care, or was it all pretend?
Why find me now?
The words are caught by the lump in my throat.

Chapter Fourteen

Prince Aries

Rory pretends to sleep. His body is too still, his heart too fast. Ayna drifts off first, his legs twitching as he starts to dream. I hear the soft scuff of his hooves on stray stones.

I stay quiet, watching Rory more than the woods. I hear the moment his breathing changes, softening into the slow, deep breaths of true sleep. His face seems younger now, more like the Ruari of my memories.

My steps are silent as I enter the henge.

I sink down onto my belly on the grass beside him, close enough that I can feel his breath on my skin. It is warm and smells faintly of mint. I breathe it into my lungs—breathe *him* into my lungs.

His hair halos around his head, curls lying gently on the bedroll and creeping into the grass. I shouldn't do it...I *know* that I shouldn't. He's always hated my little pranks and we are not children anymore. But I want to see that fire again.

He's never respected me, not as a man and not as a prince. I used to think fear would be the next best thing. I close my eyes and wonder when that changed. I don't remember... It's as if one day, I just woke up and didn't want him to be afraid anymore. Instead, I wanted to feel his warm thighs spreading beneath me, his soft skin against mine... And, after ages of careful planning, subtle manipulations, and earnest fawning, I'd gotten my wish—just for him to flee from me.

Now, it is my turn to get angry.

I'd done everything for him, everything he asked and even what he hadn't. I'd stopped my pranks, even stopped my friends from playing theirs, despite the loss of respect it had bought me. I'd treated him better than any of the Borrowed could have ever dreamed of.

I'd bargained Faerie for sweet-smelling flowers and clover honey. I'd left him gifts of lavender and sweet cream. He, who had been lowest of the low, and I, a Prince. He'd given me one night inside his body, then fled. For a while, I'd believed him stolen, and in my anger, I'd laid accusation at the feat of a dozen faeries. We'd fought—to their death and dismemberment—but it had gotten me no closer to finding him.

With no one to blame and no ransom to pay, I'd started instead to believe him dead from my magic, his body spirited away.

It was Marik who'd told me the truth in the end.

Ruari resented the care the faeries had given him and stepped into a Tear the first chance he got.

And since Marik was a faerie, I knew he could not lie. Ruari had left me without so much as a goodbye.

My old anger flares hot, bursting out of me in a wave of magic. Freed from my flesh, it takes on a life of its own, tangling Rory's hair into twisted knots tighter than I've ever seen. The ends coil in weeds and along the lengthy spines of grass, pinning Rory's head to the bedroll. If he were to try to sit up, they would not allow it.

He doesn't wake up.

I almost feel guilty.

* * * *

Rory

In dreams, a memory comes.

The yellow grass, soft as spider-silk, curls its blades around my bare feet. I am lying, nude as a newborn, on my back at the very heart of the small meadow. Neglected, she'd been, or so the grass had whispered when I'd stumbled into the ovular glade. Too small to appeal to the faeries with their greed and pride.

What deterred the fae was the very thing that drew me in. Here, I could be alone with my thoughts and worries. None to stumble on me, to tease or poke or...or flirt. I feel my cheeks warm more than the sunlight warrants at the thought.

Never had I – a mortal, a Borrowed boy with no worth beyond the music my hands could make, which is none, or could be stolen from my soul – expected to be at the center of a faerie's attempt at seduction. If not for the bard's songs or the playwright's drama, I might not have even recognized the act for what it was.

Aodhan is courting me. The little gifts he's leaving at the foot of my bedroll for me to find each morning, though he's always fled his bedroom before I wake to find them, the sudden wariness of my usual tormentors, his bright smile whenever he spots me, they've all led me to this belief.

But it must be another of his pranks, right? A new way to humble me? Is it his plan to convince me of his care, lure me to trust him, then leave me again in the mud and weeds? I still remember that time when we were younger. I'd been nearly half the height I've grown to now and he'd still had his faeling buttons where one day his antlers would grow – now, they are forkhorns, four sharp spikes on a narrow rack.

He'd convinced me to play a game with him and I'd been happy to be included – until I'd realized the game he wished to play was no game at all. He'd been bored and with his friends, they'd planned a Hunt. Seven faeries, three Borrowed.

I shudder at the memory and open my eyes. The sky is bright but I can blame the stinging on the sun. I still hear Elva's screams in my nightmares. They'd caught her first, sending an arrow through her belly. They'd pinned her to the old oak and tormented her for hours, feeding her hot coals disguised as apples and letting the crows peck at her eyes and entrails. She'd been alive through it all.

I'd been forced to watch from my hiding space, curled up shoulder to knee in the too-tight hollow of the rabbit burrow. Of all the Borrowed, I was the youngest and by far the scrawniest. My master the prince fed me scraps from his mother's table when I was good – but I was rarely good.

It is hard to remember the headstrong child I used to be before that night.

They didn't know I watched them. Perhaps if they did, they would have been kinder, killed her quicker…but perhaps not. Aodhan at least had gotten bored of the torture quicker than the others and left them to their play, heading off the path and deeper into the woods with only Soren, his servant, at his side.

If my hiding spot had been worse, if the scent of dead bunnies hadn't covered the stench of my fear, Aodhan would not have stopped my slaughter. It could have been me on that tree in place of Elva, or it could have been me who died on

Aodhan's sword just moments before the safety of first dawn – the Hunt ended with morning light on the third day.

Instead, I'd spent three nights and two days in the burrow, so dehydrated I didn't have tears left to cry, before he'd found me. He'd laughed as he dragged me out and paraded me through the castle, all the while proclaiming me, 'his' Borrowed, the best prey! And the next morning, he'd forgotten, moved on to fresh sports.

I could never forget, even if, somehow along the way, I'd learned to forgive.

The memory lingers as I wake. It's faded by time and leftover magic, a bite with no teeth.

Sunlight is warm where it kisses my cheeks and though my body is sore from the hard ground, the bedroll helped soften my aches and pains. I don't open my eyes immediately. For the first time in what seems like forever, I feel safe and calm. The air smells like fresh grass.

I'm smiling when I open my eyes – until I go to sit up and realize I'm pinned in place. My hair is star-fished out around my head, pulling at my scalp painfully as I try to move.

"Aries!" My rage-filled scream bursts out of me with enough volume to send birds exploding into the air from a nearby tree, but Aries just laughs.

It is the same casually hurtful sound from my memories, proof if there ever was that he has not changed enough.

His face appears in my field of vision above me, lips twisted in a smirk, eyes twinkling. For a second, I see two of him – the Aries of my youth, long-limbed and slender, and the Aries of now, glamoured into a mountain of a man. They merge into one.

"Morning, sleeping beauty," he teases, his voice like an echo of the past. It twists knives into my heart.

My magic—a crooked, not-quite-human, not-quite-faerie snarl—bursts out of me like a briefcase bomb. Less deadly, perhaps, but no less powerful. It shoves Aries away from me, sending him flying through the air and into one of the standing stones with enough force that the monolith spiderwebs with cracks.

Even Ayna catches the edge of my anger. It sends him rolling several feet in his bedroll toward the edge of the clearing.

And before it fades, it loosens Aries' hold on me, freeing my hair from the tangled knots trying to keep me pinned. I push myself to my feet.

Aries is frozen against the stone for the length of a breath, then his glamour fractures, flickering twice before it disappears. The mountain of a man is gone, leaving in his place a willowy Black man. He is tall but slender and he looks so much like my memory of him I feel for a moment like I've been dragged back in time. Then my eyes lock on his antlers and I'm settled again in the present.

They no longer look like they belong on a yearling—an elk would be jealous of their breadth. They are elegant and deadly.

He stares at me, silent, and his surprise is palpable—like static in the air. Then he straightens. His skin flickers for a moment, like he's trying to pull his glamour back on, but sputters and fades.

"I am no fainting princess, no damsel in distress," I hiss at him through bared and suddenly sharp teeth. "And I will not let you rape my mind or body for your amusement."

He looks stunned by my outburst but as soon as the vulgar word — *rape* — slips out of my mouth his shock turns to rage. He furrows his eyebrows but the expression does not look so fierce on his true face. Petulant is what he looks, what he *is*.

"I am not a rapist," he spits at me as he stalks forward but I hold my ground.

"What would you call a man who takes advantage of another in their sleep? Who uses their power to make another feel small and scared? You may not have fucked my body *this time* but you certainly did not hesitate to fuck *with* it," I growl the words but they start to muddle, uttered from a mouth full of too many teeth. I taste copper as I bite the soft flesh of my tongue hard enough to bleed.

Aries stills, finally wary. "It was just a joke. I didn't mean…"

"To make me feel weak? To remind me that, as always, I am in your power and bound," I touch my hand — complete with claws — to the center of my chest where our withered bond still faintly pulses, "by your will?"

He opens his mouth to speak but the words choke off in his throat. Like all faeries, he cannot tell a lie.

"You promised me that you would never do it again," I whisper, and the admission saps me of my anger. Only sadness remains. I am weary to my bones. The teeth in my mouth start to loosen. I spit them, one bloody, needle-sharp bone at a time, to the dirt, until only my dull, flat, *human* teeth are left.

"You have become an oath-breaker, Aries-who-once-was-Aodhan," I murmur, turning my back on him and crouching to fold up my bedroll. My hands shake as I tie the green ribbon around its center.

"I...remember no such promise," Aries answers, his own voice little more than a whisper. It doesn't sound as if he's moved. Ayna is silent as well, only a brief rustle of the cloth to betray his presence, though I feel the weight of his eyes.

"Is that what matters?" I wonder, hands stilling. "The memory? If I make a promise and then forget it, does the promise die?"

"I don't know." His voice is strangled. "We are bound by our oaths. Faerie would never allow us to forget them..." He doesn't sound certain.

"Something tells me Faerie is a little preoccupied right now," I answer darkly. I grab my bedroll and stand. We don't have time to debate philosophy now. "We need to move. Dawn has broken."

Chapter Fifteen

Prince Aries

It has been many years since I've felt shame as strong as this.

Had I made Rory a promise? And had I broken it? I truly don't remember and that, more than anything else I've seen since returning to Faerie, frightens me. *Oath-breaker,* he'd named me. *Is he right?*

Rory is not a faerie. He is not bound by a covenant of truth. Still, there was a ring of honesty to his voice. I do not believe he is lying, but neither was I.

It is a mystery. Since returning to Faerie, I have found too many mysteries.

Rory leaves the henge behind him and reenters the forest. I follow, and Ayna is quiet on my heels. I look to him and see him staring at Rory's back, his expression…considering. I sense an undercurrent of his thoughts from the invisible bridle around my wrist.

"I do not believe you would find him an easy victim," I say softly, glancing between the water and Rory.

"I have never felt the urge to drown someone so strongly," Ayna answers, his voice a breathy whine. "Is it him or is it this place?"

"Perhaps some mixture of both," I acknowledge, then lay a hand upon his shoulder to halt him. We both stop walking. "You will harm neither hide nor hair, nor blood, flesh or bone of that boy's body. Do you understand?" I let my words fill with the strength of my geas, powered by the bridle that bends him to my will.

Ayna whimpers, shoulders curling, but he bows his head. "I…do not truly wish to harm him, I don't think."

It is not a lie but phrased in such a way that I can tell even he is not sure he believes the words. "And now you cannot," I say gently, looking toward Rory. The distance between us has grown — both literally and figuratively — so I start to walk again.

As we catch up to Rory's shadow, I find myself wondering…what memory did Faerie steal?

Perhaps it meant more to me than I'd understood.

* * * *

If I'd been paying better attention, I might have noticed the trap before we crossed it. Instead, it caught us in the loop unaware. I couldn't even honestly say how long we'd been snared. Minutes? Hours? Nearly the whole day?

If Ayna hadn't spoken, how long would we have wandered in circles?

"I'm going crazy. I swear we've passed that tree already," he mutters under his breath as he glares at a birch tree with a crooked trunk.

It's not until he points it out that I catch the glimmer of gold threads weaving along the path. Magic, hastily laid but strong enough to catch us.

"Damn it," I curse and without thinking, I grab for Rory's arm to stop him.

He flinches away and pins me with a glare. "Hands off," he snaps and I release him immediately and clear my throat.

"We're going in circles," I say instead of speaking out loud any of my numerous thoughts—only one of which was an apology.

Rory narrows his eyes and I can tell that, at first, he doesn't believe me. Or, at least he doesn't *want* to believe me. He follows Ayna's gaze to the tree, then curses as well.

"It's Faerie magic, can you break it?" he asks, voice sharp. There's no apology in his eyes.

I turn my eyes to the gold glimmer again. "Probably. It's weak and freshly laid, hasn't had time to sink its roots in." Suddenly, an idea strikes. It's impulsive but right now, with that fire in his eyes...I know what I want more than anything. "Kiss me and I'll break it for you."

He stares at me, nonplussed, before his eyes spark again with anger. "Really? Chased by all the Queen's men and you...of course. Of *course*. Why would you care if we are caught?" His voice lowers at the end as if he's talking to himself and it births a bit of embarrassment in my chest, but not enough to have me back down. Besides, a bargain spoken is a bargain I can't take back.

He glares in the direction of the magic web that I know he cannot see, the one that twists the path into a never-ending circle. "Fine. Fucking *fine*." He grumbles but steps toward me. We are nearly chest to chest, face to face. Would be, if he was but a hand taller. He tips his head back, keeping his eyes open and on mine like a dare.

"I said kiss *me*," I remind him, my breath catching in my throat. Perhaps I am no better than what he called me. A shadow of shame haunts my chest but I ignore it, overwhelmed instead by the warmth of his lips on mine. They are velvet soft and yet his kiss is rough, violent. He doesn't just kiss me, he tears the very breath from my lungs.

When he releases me, he doesn't step back. Instead, with scant inches between our faces, he says quietly, "I heard you were a good cop, Aries. That you were brave and honorable." Then, there is the loud *crack* of his palm striking my face as he slaps me, too fast for me to see more than the blur of his hand. "How then can you also be such an *asshole*?"

And I realize suddenly that I don't know.

I close my eyes, but not against the pain in my cheek. The throbbing is already fading, healed by the ambient magic of Faerie. Instead, I remember my time on Earth. It is as if that Aries were a different person. He would never have thought it right to use mischief magic on an unsuspecting person, not even an enemy. He would never have bargained for a kiss from someone who so clearly didn't want one.

I can see that, but I don't understand. Trying to understand that Aries, who is me, who *was* me, and yet…somehow also not…is like trying to hold fire.

Out loud, all I can say is, "I don't know."

He looks disappointed. Lips pursed, he steps back, putting space between us. "Break the spell, Aries. We need to move quickly, before whatever caught us comes to spring their trap."

"It may be too late already," I mutter, hearing the faint sound of footsteps. Still in the distance, far enough away that I know Faerie is allowing me to hear them on purpose. She wants to warn me, which tells me whoever approaches is not a friend.

I break the trap quickly but not without cost—I grimace as it strikes back, the magic crackling toward me like a whip. I reflexively lift my arm to block its lash and a line of fire spreads from wrist to elbow. Three beads of blue blood fall to the ground and Faerie quakes in anger beneath my feet.

"*Fuck,*" Rory curses, fear on his face. His eyes are not on me—they are pointed toward our pursuer. "We need to be quick." He grabs my other arm and starts to drag me. He ignores Ayna like he's done all day but the half-breed follows anyway. Ayna's face is blank but I don't have the energy to check in with him.

At Rory's urging, we are running full tilt down the path, which grows narrower and rougher with every step.

Then, the path ends.

We have reached the borders of the Wild.

Chapter Sixteen

Rory

The path ends abruptly. Not in a natural way, overgrown by weeds or blocked by fallen trees. It ends with surgical precision, as if Faerie itself is warning us to go no further.

In front of me is a bramble of blackberries, familiar thorns so sharp they look as if they could separate flesh from bone then stitch it back together if one would only lend it some thread.

"How the fuck are we supposed to get through *that*?" It is Ayna whose voice, gritty and loud, breaks the silence, speaking the same words that I was just thinking.

"We pay the toll," Aries mumbles, and I don't think it's my imagination that his voice sounds slurred. When I meet his eyes, they are glassy, the pupils blown. A glance at his arm shows an oozing wound. Whatever magic caused it, he is still in its grip.

"Do you know what it is?" I ask. The map I'd stolen, which I'd stopped only briefly to examine, had simply said, "Enter the Wilds". It had not said how.

"Yeats had it a bit right and a bit wrong," Aries answers. Then, in a song-like voice, he says, "*Come away, o human child, to the waters and the wild, with a faery hand in hand.*" Aries smiles a strange smile and holds out his uninjured arm. "Give me your hand, human child."

I don't have time to argue that I am neither human nor a child. I take his offered hand.

And it burns like hot iron but something inside me warns me not to let go. Even though it feels like my flesh is melting off, like the heat is burning down to my very bones, I keep hold.

Aries pulls me through the bramble. I shut my eyes and whimper as the thorns come quickly at my face but I pass through as if they are mist. He releases my hand three steps later and the pain immediately vanishes. I open my eyes and see that my hand is undamaged.

I turn to the bramble that is now behind me and, though I do not like my former lover's new lover, I frown. "What of Ayna?" Hardly had the words passed my lips and Ayna, eyes closed and sweat on his brow, walks through the bramble.

He shudders once clear and opens his eyes. "Even though I could see that it wasn't real, that still *sucked*."

"We should hurry," Aries says, his voice still dreamy. "He who follows will be able to pass through, if he wishes." His lips twitch toward a frown. "Though I sense that he is just a watcher. The real danger is yet to arrive."

"I'd like to be long gone before they do," I agree. I turn away and realize that the bramble stretches, from left to right, in a line too straight to be natural, for as far as the eye can see. Now, instead of a forest, we are standing a few feet shy from the edge of a cliff.

"Have I ever mentioned that I hate heights?" Ayna says dryly.

Out of spite, I walk to the edge. I am not a fan of them myself but I refuse to agree with the younger man. I stare down at the narrow, deadly path. There is only one. "Looks like we're climbing," I say brightly, with more cheer than I feel. "Aries, can't you do anything about that arm?" I ask over my shoulder.

Then two hands hit the center of my back, sudden and hard, and I am flying over the edge.

Prince Aries

Whatever power the magic backlash held over me dissipates at the sight of Rory tumbling over the edge of the cliff. The time between Ayna's hands landing on his back and Rory falling is so short, he didn't have time to scream and I could barely suck in a breath.

I leap forward, throwing myself down on my belly. Gravel bites into my skin in the worst imitation of road rash but I barely notice. I look over the edge, holding onto the slim hope that Rory was able to grab a handhold before he fell. I can't see him. My gaze scours the narrow path, the sharp edges of the cliff, the protruding boulders and deep crevasses. I can't see him.

I roll myself to my knees, heart pounding with an angry terror. "What the *fuck*, Ayna?" I holler as I stalk toward him. With the geas I laid on him, he shouldn't have been able to do it, but he had and he did.

"I didn't hurt him," Ayna says calmly. "If he is harmed, it would be by the rocks or the ground. I didn't harm hide or hair, nor flesh or blood or bone."

There's something about his voice...about the calm, blank face...I grip his chin tight and yank his head back, staring into his glassy emerald orbs. My other hand curls around his throat. Whatever magic caught me must have snagged him as well. I see the gold glittering like a galaxy in his eyes.

Not just a charm to misdirect, then. We were *meant* to trip it, and *meant* to break it...in hopes of just this. A rider spell...it latches on to the host like a parasite and leeches their will, until they are little more than a puppet for the spellmaster.

Has it been too long for me to break?

Do you even want to break it? A fitting punishment for one who killed your old love, to live like a slave on an invisible leash, a malicious voice whispers in the back of my head.

If it hadn't, if the faerie bastard who'd laid the spell had stayed quiet, I might not have realized that the spell didn't break with my anger but went dormant...I might not have been able to cut it out of my own essence in time.

But the voice...I recognize it too clearly.

"Mother," I growl, still staring into her puppet's eyes. Inwardly, I work on unsnarling myself from her trap, cutting myself free quickly. It is not without pain—there is no way to break such a spell without pain—but I ignore the electric jolts. I need to free myself, then I can work on freeing Ayna...if such a thing is even possible.

And leave your silly little mortal in pieces to die, where he belongs, Mother's voice taunts in my head, quieter but no less painful. *Have you heard his screams before, darling? They taste like sweet honey.*

"Get out of my head," I say through clenched teeth, my hands tightening on Ayna's skin, so hard his flesh turns white around my fingers. He makes a choking sound.

I've been in his *head, son of mine.* Her voice is nearly gone, but I can feel her smugness. *And in his body... Aren't you going to come punish me, son of mine? Come home, son of mine...* Her voice fades until only echoes remain.

Her magic is gone from me but I can see it burning in Ayna. All I want is to find Rory, to cradle his broken body in my arms. How high is this cliff? How far did he fall? Is he still down there somewhere, lingering on the edge of life? Is he calling for me? *Crying* for me?

But I brought Ayna to Faerie. I took responsibility for him as soon as I accepted his bridle in place of his father. I have to try.

I sink my nails into the skin of Ayna's neck, spilling purple blood over my fingers, and with it, a connection to the core of his being. There is much debate among my kind as to whether a half-breed has a soul. Humans do, and many other magical beings, but us faeries don't. We have a core of life magic, like a battery. When we die, it dies with us.

I don't know if Ayna has a soul. The magical center of him feels much like any other faerie I've performed a pseudo-psychic surgery on. Hot to the touch, like holding on to a power line, but spiky like barbed wire. Right now, it's more gold than green.

My mother's hooks have grown deep...but not, I think, deep enough. Like an angry gardener stripping a garden to start fresh, I start to pull her weeds from his soil, pruning the gold strands away with no mercy.

What remains of his essence is battered, the green muddy, and I sense that he is in a lot of pain...a mental anguish that won't fade easily. Her hooks had gotten nowhere near as deep in me, though whether that was due to my own natural protection as a full-blooded faerie against magic, my connection to Rory's mortal soul, or some other reason is unclear. Despite that, I feel like someone has taken sandpaper to my skin then poured bleach on it. I can't imagine his pain.

I am in no mood to feel empathy either. I let him fall to the ground and he shudders. He draws in a ragged breath and immediately starts to cough. I turn my back on him and stalk to the edge of the cliff, staring down.

I can't see his body, alive or...otherwise. Then I blink and the image wavers.

A glamour...I'm looking at a glamour.

Chapter Seventeen

Rory

I fall for what seems like ever but is in reality only a scant few seconds. Then, I land in the dirt. It billows up around me in a dusty cloud that clogs my nose and sends me into a fit of coughing. When it finally clears, I open my stinging eyes and stare above me.

How far had I fallen? Apparently, about five feet. Enough to skin my hands and knees when I landed, but nowhere near as long as it should have been, considering the height of the cliff.

A glamour, I realize. I push myself to my feet and go to the wall, planning to climb it back up so I could scream at whichever one of those mother *fuckers* thought they could shove me over the cliff—*had Aries known it was a glamour and thought it would be a funny joke? Or had Ayna* not *known it and thought it an easy way to remove the competition?*—but as soon as I touch the wall, something shocks me.

I jerk back and glare at it, then try to touch it again. The shock is stronger this time. "Well, fuck you too," I grumble and drop down onto my ass, careful to stay away from the rocks. I slip the strap to the quiver off my shoulder and pull it in into my lap, then – carefully, this time – slip my hand in between the arrows.

I pull out the map and shift the quiver to give myself room to unfurl it. I run my fingers over the areas we'd left – the Queen's castle, the Queen's Forest, the two largest areas of the Sidhe court's land – and trail it to the Wilds – or, as it reads on the map, the wildlands. If the Sidhe lands were the size of a plum, then the wildlands were a pomegranate. The Unsidhe lands were a smudged suggestion of space north of the Sleeping Giants' Mountain Range.

I trail my finger over the map, following what I think might be the best path. A day, maybe day-and-a-half, trek through the aptly labeled 'desert'. Nothing in the wildlands has been named, I notice. After the desert, there's a stretch of 'dead woods', then a 'loch' at the foothills of the mountains.

And over the mountains, safety.

I try to memorize as many landmarks as I can while I wait for the two bastards above me to make their way down. A large part of me is torn on waiting…I could leave now, without them. Maybe I would be safer. Every rational part of me is *certain* I would be safer.

I don't move.

I don't think I can stomach walking away from Aries, even if he was the one who shoved me. I can't believe he would have done it if he thought it would bring me harm… Out loud, I scold myself, "But you never thought he'd Hunt you, either. You never thought he'd leave you to the Court to toy with. That's your problem, Rory boy." I take a deep breath and shove the map back into the quiver, slinging it over my shoulder as I stand. "You never *think*."

I've taken three steps when I hear a *thud* behind me, then a second, less graceful one. "I see you decided to follow," I say dryly, trying to hide the odd mixture of emotions I'm feeling — *anger, joy, fear, relief.*

"*Rory.*" Aries says my name in a way I can't ignore — his voice cracks with emotion I hesitate to name. I turn to look at him and a small sliver of my anger melts. I don't believe that he could push me off the cliff and then look like that, so it must have been…

I turn my gaze to Ayna. He looks sick, like he's been fighting off the flu. I see the ring of bruises on his neck and chin, the dried blood. I decide not to comment. I look back to Aries and fake a smile. "Now that we're all accounted for, we should push on. Keep an eye out for water, we'll hit the desert in a few miles."

"Rory," he says my name again and steps toward me, lifting his hand toward my face as if to caress it.

I can't deal with his emotional meltdown or whatever the hell this is right now. Not if I want to keep my own composure. I can't afford to break now — panic attacks tend to come with blackouts or memories of things I *wish* I'd blacked out.

"Don't," I say, voice sharp. He flinches but his hand drops.

"I'll follow you," he says, and maybe he means that he will walk when I do. For some reason, though, I sense he means something more. There's a weight to the words, a promise.

I ignore it.

For now, anyway. Maybe later, when I am safe, I will take the words out and examine them, run them through my mind like an artist examines a clay sculpture. Examine it for imperfections, for cracks and divots.

We find a small stream. It's barely ankle deep and nearly as much silt as water, but old memories surface quickly. Aries passes me a waterskin from his bag. I recognize it. I remember the puca he killed to harvest its bladder.

I never cared about drinking from it back then, but now, after centuries in the mortal world with its plastic containers and hygiene, I feel queasy about using it. I don't, however, have a choice. It's the bladder or nothing.

Later, I know I will regret choosing nothing so for now, I hold the end of my shirt over the nozzle and use it as a makeshift filter as I fill the waterskin. When it's full, I cap it and hook the carrying strap through the loop on my pants. It's a chilly weight against my hip. My shirt is muddy and damp now, but hopefully, it will dry fast in the heat of the desert.

Aries wastes no time filling his but when Ayna squats to fill his, Aries seems to hesitate. He comes to a decision quickly. I watch as his shoulders straighten—even slender as he is without his glamour, he has a *presence*.

"Ayna," Aries says, and the kelpie freezes. "The desert is no place for a kelpie, full-blooded or not. There will be no water or rest for you."

Ayna stares at the stream, shoulders hunching forward, and he doesn't speak.

"I want you to follow this stream to its source. Lay a fake trail to cover for us, then return to Faerie. I'll try to find you when I've delivered Rory safely to the Unsidhe," Aries decides.

"What of the bridle?" Ayna asks. I don't know what he speaks of, but Aries seems to.

"It will stay safe with me. You will not need it, nor feel any ill effects from our separation so long as you follow my orders while we are apart. Your father, after all, has lived away from my side for many years." Aries' voice is surprisingly gentle.

For the first time, I have an inkling that perhaps they were not lovers after all.

I am still happy to watch his shoulders slump as he walks away.

I am not a nice man.

Chapter Eighteen

Rory

"It'll be too hot for the cloak," Aries tells me, holding out his hand. "I can put it in my bag."

"No—" I bite off the 'thank you' that almost slips out. My time on Earth had softened the memories of faerie customs a bit too much.

Aries waits a moment like he expects me to finish but when I don't say anything else, he adds, "It's going to be too hot to wear and too heavy to carry."

He's right. I *know* he's right, but I don't want to admit it. Partly out of stubbornness—I don't want him to carry anything of mine—but mostly, I'm worried he won't give it back. He'll turn me over to his brethren or...or leave me stranded out here or something. I might not want the cloak in the desert, but I'll need it to avoid freezing to death in the mountains.

Grumbling under my breath, I take off the quiver of arrows, resting it against my legs so I can strip off the heavy cloak and shove it at him. I replace the quiver while he's still shoving the cloak — carefully, I'll admit, but I'm not feeling generous — into his pack. Before I can start walking, Aries says something else...and I know there's *no* way I heard him correctly. I face him again. "What?"

"I'll need to carry you," he repeats, proving that I heard him right the first time.

"Not going to happen," I answer immediately. There's no way I'm putting myself at his mercy like that.

"It makes no sense to have Ayna lay a fake trail if ours is easily found. Faerie will hide my steps if I ask her, but I can't make her hide yours," Aries explains, his voice calm but not apologetic.

I hate that he's right.

My relationship with Faerie has always been...difficult. She's as likely to grow flashing neon signs pointing toward me as to help me hide. A capricious bitch, that's what she is.

Awkwardly, I step toward him. "How..." I start to ask but he lifts me before I can finish, cradling me in his arms like a child...or a bride. The quiver bangs into his side but he doesn't even seem to notice. Aries may appear willowy but he's stronger than me. I stiffen and clutch at his neck. "If you drop me, I swear to the gods..."

"I don't believe in any god." Aries grins, his teeth sharp and white. Now I remember the many times he'd mocked the faeries who still clung to the old ways, worshipping the Horned God who hadn't been seen in the green spaces in living memory.

"That's because you think you *are* a god," I say dryly. He laughs and starts to walk without disputing it.

I try to ignore the way his arms feel around me, staring out at the surrounding land instead. The sparse grass and gravel from the banks of the narrow stream have given way to scorched earth. In the span of just moments, it's grown unbearably hot. My linen shirt sticks to my skin and sweat is trailing in itchy rivers down my spine. A salty bead drips down my forehead and into my left eye.

Cursing, I try to wipe it clear but feel like I'm doing nothing except rubbing it around. I find myself wishing I'd given Aries the sword and quiver to carry as well, because even that small weight is dragging me down.

Aries, of course, looks perfectly fine. He denies it, but I still believe the faeries retain at least some of the characteristics of the flowers they're birthed from. I wasn't there for Aries' blossoming, but I'd heard he was formed in the bud of a Heart to Heart.

I tear my gaze away from his glistening face and back to our surroundings. The ground is dry and brittle and the cracks look deep. Too dry for dust, I notice.

"Take a drink," Aries says, his voice loud in the otherwise still air.

"You're not my boss," I grump, but I fumble for the bladder at my waist and take one anyway. Not because he told me to, but because my mouth is parched. It doesn't do much to quench my thirst though. The water is hot and gritty.

"Good boy," Aries says, mouth splitting in a grin.

"I'm not a dog," I growl, tightly closing the bladder again while I glare at him.

"Woof," he barks back and his expression is so playful, I can't stop my lips from twitching. I force my eyes back to our surroundings. The cracked dirt, the hay mirage dancing on the horizon—though maybe it's real. Who's to say that Faerie doesn't have oceans in the heart of her deserts? I could swear I hear the gulls.

Looking anywhere is better than at Aries. With that smile and his eyes…he could drown me in them if I give him the chance. His arms are like brands against my skin.

Suddenly, I feel like I can't breathe.

"Put me down," I blurt, chest tight. "I can walk from here."

"Not yet," Aries answers, his voice calm. Too calm, compared to mine, as if my presence in his arms doesn't bother him at all. He tightens them around me.

"I don't think anyone would follow us this far," I reply, and even to my ears my voice sounds desperate. Who has he turned me into?

"What's that saying?" Aries asks, and when I look at him, he quirks his eyebrow. "Better safe than sorry? Besides, it's not like this is the first time you've had my arms around you." His grin is smug as he adds, "and I doubt it will be the last."

I want to hit him. Unfortunately, I think he'd like it.

Instead, I reach up and twist his ear…hard. He drops me with a yelp and cups the tender tip in his hand, his expression stunned. It's worth the hard landing to see it on his royal face.

I rub my hip, where I'm sure a bruise is already forming, and stand, brushing the dirt off my pants with a smug grin of my own. "I'm not a child, nor am I your bride. Next time I say, 'put me down,' you may want to remember this feeling."

"You didn't have to go for the *ear*," Aries whines.

"Next time, I'll go for the balls," I suggest. I swear he goes pale. It's not a good look on him, his dark skin going gray. I quirk my own eyebrow and add, "Try using those pretty ears of yours next time, hm-mm? Faerie made them so big for a reason."

Now that I'm standing on my own two—bare—feet, I'm regretting already my hasty action to get down. The ground is hard and hot, nothing like the soft sand of a beach. Instead, it's reminiscent of summer blacktop. Great for a makeshift greenhouse, not so great for sensitive skin. Pebbles are sharp against my soles.

"I don't suppose you have any boots in that magic bag of yours?" I ask wistfully, but I'm not surprised when he shakes his head. "Of course not," I mutter. Faeries may be clotheshorses, but shoes were a different matter. I would guess he was only wearing them now out of a habit born from his time on Earth. Humans didn't abide with bare feet like the fae did.

I try to ignore the painful heat as I start to walk. I struggle to hide my winces but don't succeed. Aries almost grabs me at least twice but each time stops himself with a hand lifted to his ear.

We make it about ten feet before I give in. "Fine. I *guess* you can carry me. But *not* because I can't walk! It'll just be…safer to keep my footsteps hidden. In case someone is following. Which they probably *aren't*," I stress, unwilling to think about what we will do if someone is, "but better safe than sorry."

Aries seems relieved as he scoops me up again. I try not to think about how we look. Like…like I'm some damsel in distress from a literal fairy tale and he my knight in shining armor. Maybe I am in distress…fleeing, as I am, from a bitch of a faerie queen, but I'm *not* a damsel, damn it! And Aries is no knight. Without his glamour, he's no bigger than I am.

I don't ask him why he's not wearing it. I'm afraid if I remind him, he'll pull it on like a cloak and I'll lose this…whatever this is.

The silence is uncomfortable, growing more so the longer we walk. It's a heavy, awkward kind of quiet that makes my chest tight and my fingers want to fidget. I don't realize I'm biting my nails until I taste copper. I yank my hands away from my mouth and wipe my bloody fingers on Aries' shirt. He glances at the smear of red for a moment, then gives me a look, but he doesn't protest.

I only have one shirt. It may be sweaty and dirty, but it's the only one I have and it's *mine*. I don't plan on adding blood to the nasty mix. I can't stomach the thought of wearing his clothes. Not when once, it was all I'd ever dreamed of. My princeling — I freeze on the thought and swallow around the lump forming in my throat. I force myself to rephrase the thought.

The princeling would certainly have spare clothing he could change into, if my blood bothered him so much.

The silence breaks me first.

"So," I blurt, voice louder than I intended. I scramble to think of something to ask that isn't about his glamour and won't draw his attention to anything I'd rather not speak of. I clear my throat and say, quieter this time, "When did you join the Bureau?"

Aries blinks his well-deep eyes at me. "The Bureau?"

It's a random question, the first I dragged onto my tongue, but now that I've asked it, I realize that I truly am curious. Of all the versions of Aries I'd known — Aodhan, Prince of War, Prince of Charm, Prince of

Mischief and Schemes—I'd never thought I'd see him with a badge, playing at law and order.

"You were never much of a rule follower," I elaborate. "I'd have thought you'd try on being a lawyer, maybe… Could be fun to twist the truth to your benefit, I could see how you'd enjoy the challenge of it. I could see you playing politician, even. Wouldn't have guessed cop."

"Agent," he corrects me, and his eyes go dull. "You don't know me anymore, Ruar—Rory."

"And whose fault is that?" I mutter, anger spiking to life again. "Never mind. This was stupid. I should know better than to think you and I could be anything but enemies."

"I'm not your enemy," Aries corrects me, his voice ringing with truth. "But I refuse to bear the whole of the blame for what we've turned into." His gaze draws me in and leaves me feeling weak. "I joined the Bureau after my last lover passed."

I try to hide my flinch but I know I don't succeed. His eyes, as always, see too much of me. I have not been celibate since we parted but none of my partners have been my choice. To know he's had a lover—several, I'm guessing, since he said 'last' lover—just hammers in the knowledge that I was never special to him.

*But he came for you…*a small voice in the back of my head whispers.

I ruthlessly stomp it down. *He came,* I agree, *but not out of love.* I don't know why he came, but I know he has an ulterior motive. Maybe duty, maybe curiosity. Maybe to spite his mother. I don't know which and I can't allow myself to care.

Aries keeps talking, unaware—or uncaring—of the turmoil his words spurred in me. "He was an analyst with the Bureau. I thought, of all people, *he* would be safe. He wasn't an artist or an actor. He hated the opera, *detested* the ballet, and I couldn't get him within a mile of a gym or athletic field. Passionless, I'd thought. The perfect man for someone like me."

I stay quiet, listening. I've never stopped to think what that would be like…knowing that anyone I love was doomed to die because of me. Though…the only person I've ever loved is holding me now, and there have been days where I dreamed of his death, of what his blood would feel like beneath my nails and in my teeth.

Aries sighs and the violent image dissipates. "I didn't realize that his true passion was his work. He solved sixteen homicides and laid the groundwork for solving another dozen before he worked himself to death."

Aries gives a choked laugh. "I didn't notice how thin he'd gotten until it was too late. He'd been spending so many hours at the Bureau, we'd been passing each other like ships."

The question slips out of me before I can catch it. "And you weren't angry that his passion for the Bureau meant more to him than his love for you?"

Aries flinches like I struck him. "Maybe he loved the Bureau more than me, or maybe my curse pushed him that way. I don't know. I do know that he was the first of my lovers who died for something bigger than him. It wasn't for a piece of canvas or a slab of stone, or…or fame or fortune. He was saving people's lives. And he would have kept saving people's lives if he'd never met me."

"So you joined to finish what he started…" I murmur.

I can't imagine loving someone enough to change who I am at my very core. Not again. Not ever again.

"Hm-mmm," he hums in agreement, then goes silent. There is pain written all over his face.

I want to ask him where his pain was when he left me, but I know the answer. He never loved me. If he did, I'd have withered away and died like his other lovers. Instead, like a weed, I've managed to survive despite everything this world has thrown at me.

I look away from Aries. I don't want to see the evidence of his love for another man, not when I have no choice but to sit here, cradled in his cold arms.

You don't care anyway, I tell myself. *You got over him a long time ago. This is just...residual emotions stirred up by a stressful situation.*

Fortunately, Faerie decides to throw something in our path to distract me from my melancholy.

Unfortunately, we might not survive it.

Chapter Nineteen

Prince Aries

I can tell Rory is upset by my words, and something about his obvious anger stirs mine as well. What right does he have to be angry? So I took a new lover, a dozen new lovers? He left me. *He* left *me.*

Before I can act on my rage, Faerie saves me from saying something I'll regret. The still, dead air starts to stir. I notice it first in the fluttering of Rory's copper hair, then sand bites at my skin. I look away from him quickly and stare in horror at the growing shadow on the horizon.

Sandstorm.

I glare down at the cracked dirt in disgust. "Are you shitting me?" I curse, and I know Faerie hears me. She shakes the ground with mocking laughter. *You'll thank me later*, I sense her reply.

Rory is staring at the dark, steadily growing smudge on the horizon, horror in his eyes. "We have to run," he urges, fear in his voice.

"We can't outrun *that*," I immediately argue, setting him on his feet and dropping to my knees. I rip my bag off my back and stick my arm in, fumbling around until I feel the rough hide of my tent beneath my fingers. "Help me," I urge as I yank it out, unrolling the fabric quickly. "Grab the ends and get them staked." I toss the stakes, the antler bone still sharp, to his side, then grab the collapsible wooden pole from the bag.

Thank Faerie for muscle memory. I haven't had to pitch a tent in centuries, but it goes up quicker than I hoped and is sturdier than I remember. It should weather the storm, unless Faerie decides to send a Black Blizzard our way.

I have to trust that she won't. Whatever she thinks to gain with this, I have to believe she doesn't want us dead. If she did, she could open a pit below our very feet with much less effort.

I hold open the tent flap. "In, quickly," I order, and for once, Rory doesn't argue. He scrambles inside and I follow him. "Help me tie." I grab for the leather thongs. I start at the bottom. They come in pairs, one on the flap and one on the tent itself. I let my magic strengthen the knots. Rory is slower. Our hands meet two-thirds of the way up.

Outside, the wind is howling. The sides of the tent are vibrating with its intensity and I fear we may blow away. I force down my worries and fumble around in the bag again until I pull out one of my spare night shirts. The silk weave is tighter than linen. A quick slice from my dagger has the shirt in two pieces. I pass him the larger.

"Wrap it around your mouth and nose. If the tent fails, you'll need it." I do the same with the other piece of fabric. I feel silly with the arm hole flapping by my left ear, but better silly than dead. Immediately, it's hard to breathe, the fabric sticking to my mouth, growing damp from my breath.

Rory is slower to wrap his face but, in the end, he does it without protest.

Now, all we can do is wait.

* * * *

Time in Faerie is fluid and hard to measure, but if we were back on Earth, I'd hazard to bet we've been weathering the storm — *no pun intended,* I snicker to myself — for almost an hour, with no sign of it lessening.

Rory has been sitting tense on the other side of the tent, as far from me as he could get, the entire time. He'd taken off the quiver and his sword but left them right at his side, easy to grab. His eyes are wide, though I can't tell if he's afraid of the storm, of our pursuers...or of me. It's not the first time he's looked at me with those eyes. I used to love that look, the mixture of terror and keen awareness. Like the fear made sure that every molecule in his body is laser focused on me.

Now...the fear does something else to me. I don't want him to be afraid, though I couldn't pinpoint why, or when that feeling started. I sense that I've felt that way for a long while, but...it also feels new. Fresh.

Unexpected.

He meets my eyes and lightning courses between our bodies. I know — I don't know how, but it's as clear to me as summer rain — that if I touch my skin to his, I'll burn. I want it. I want to feel the heat of his body, the way it would form to mine. A perfect match.

I've taken many a lover in the millennia I've lived, both in this world and the other, but none have ever compared to the single night I spent with him.

The memory sparks to life in his eyes, consuming me.

The glade smells of growing things.

I stand at its edge, my bare feet swallowed by dew damp grass. Shadows cradle me in their silence as I watch the newest object of my fascination. I've tried not to want him, but ever since that day by the water —

What day by the water? It feels important, a tipping point. A crossroads, but all I find is fog. Was this the price I paid to return here? I wonder, for the first time, if I should have sought out the troll instead.

The memory drags me back.

Ever since that day by the water, I've been at his mercy, whether he knows it or not. He is a sweet-smelling flower, and I am the bee, here to steal the nectar from his petals. I fear without it I will die.

Ruari is basking, nude, on a smooth gray stone in a patch of sunlight at the center of the glade. His pale skin is kissed with golden warmth. For a moment, I am jealous of the suns. He's fashioned a pillow from a bed of moss and purple wildflowers. It cushions his head. His fiery hair is a glowing halo against the muted green and violet.

I want to go to him, to claim his flesh with mine, but fear stops me. Not that he will harm me — no mortal, not even a wild one like him, has a chance at damaging my body. I trained beneath the keen eye of the great Arteria himself. Only my friend Anik comes close to rivaling my skills, as Arteria's second apprentice.

No, my fear is that he will flee from me. Or, worse, laugh. I can bear many things — pain, boredom — but not his mockery. For the first time, I need more than just passing fun from a partner. If he spurs me, I fear I will die.

If he doesn't, then I fear he will.

How many mortals have become my playthings only to wither away? I've never cared before. Never bothered to watch the way the light died from their eyes as the muse I left in them burned them away. I'd already moved on to the next by the time Faerie swallowed their bodies.

Before I can talk myself into moving – either toward his blissful form or back to my empty cottage I call home – someone else moves first.

Anik, my dear friend, and his loyal lackeys Alberich and Anwynn.

I frown, wondering why they are here, bothering my Ruari, without me. It is a pastime of ours, pranking Ruari. Always mine more than theirs, though. Anwynn and Alberich have their own favorite pet to torture, a dark-haired waif of a boy who cries like an angel. Anik doesn't have a plaything. My mother keeps him too busy.

Ruari notices them only moments after I do. His whole body goes tense – gods, I love the way his smooth skin tightens over wiry muscles. Unlike many of my brethren, I don't believe in the Horned God, but if I did, I'd say he gifted me with the finest specimen to toy with.

For me to toy with, not my friends.

"What do we have here, boys?" Anik says, his voice a mocking drawl.

"I don't know, Anik." Alberich laughs and pulls out a dagger. Silver, it catches the light. "But why don't we find out?"

Anwynn is the only one who looks uncomfortable. His eyes dart to the tree line. His gaze skims past me, unseeing. "Maybe we should wait. I don't think Aodhan – "

"Feck Aodhan. We don't need him to make the little shite cry."

"You don't?" I ask, voice dry as I step out of the shadows, on the other side of the glade from my friends. Ruari is between us, spine hunched and shoulders tense where he waited on the rock. "And here I thought I gave my orders. No one makes Ruari cry without me."

I step closer, until my shadow falls on Ruari's body. Any humor I may have had in my voice, I strip away. I am deadly serious when I say, "With my blood, I claim thee." *Now my dagger is in my hand and before any can blink, I slice the flesh of my palm. My blood drips onto Ruari's chest, staining him blue.* "What you do unto him, you have done to me."

Anik just chuckles and puts his knife away. "Another time, Aodhan."

"Hm-mmm," *I hum, noncommittal.* "Tell my mother I say 'hello' when you see her, why don't you."

Anger flashes hot over Anik's face. "Well played, **friend**." *He melts back into the shadows, the twins only a step behind him. When I am certain that Ruari and I are alone, I put my knife away.*

Ruari huffs and slides off the rock, seeming careful to keep from turning his back to me. Even after protecting him from my friends, he's still wary. He lifts a hand to his chest, wiping the blood – my blood – from his skin.

A growl starts in my throat too fast for me to smother it. He flinches at the sound. I lift my hand, slowly, until my still-bleeding palm cradles his face.

"Don't be afraid," *I murmur.*

"I'm not afraid," *he lies. I always know when he's lying. It's a gift from Faerie. That, and he always bites his lip afterward.*

"It's okay," *I say, and because I'm a faerie, I cannot lie. He has the right to his fear. I've certainly done enough over his life to earn it honestly.* "I'm not going to hurt you."

"Not going to hurt me **now**," *Ruari clarifies.*

"Not going to hurt you –" *I try to say ever but the word catches in my throat. Apparently, Faerie believes that at some point in the future, I will hurt him. Pain twists in my chest.* "Tonight," *I say instead.* "I don't **want** to hurt you ever."

That, at least, is true.

"You aren't going to hurt me tonight," *Ruari repeats, and the tension in his body slowly dissipates.* "So...if you aren't *going to hurt me, Princeling, what* are *you going to do to me?"*

"Whatever you'll let me."

"You're staring," Rory's voice startles me out of the memory and I blink. The tent—and Rory—come back into focus.

"You're beautiful," I say without thinking. "When did you cut your hair?"

His brows lower, darkening his green eyes. "When I realized keeping it long made me a target on the streets. Half the men thought I was a girl and then got pissed when I wasn't. The other half...well, I'd have preferred anger."

I know exactly what he means. I saw a lot once I joined the Bureau. More than I wanted to. "Were you on the streets long?" I ask, genuinely curious.

Rory drops his eyes. "What's it matter to you?"

"You matter to me," I admit. "I want to know everything."

"No. You don't."

Chapter Twenty

Rory

I don't even want to think of those days. When I painted those murals to lock away memories, half of them had been from *after* I fled Faerie. I had thought, after the pranks and mischief I'd gone through there, I'd be prepared for anything Earth could throw at me.

I'd been wrong, more naïve than a mortal child. I'd learned better. It hurt, the learning process. The scars may have healed but I can still remember where each one would have been, if my inner monster hadn't healed them.

I lift my eyes to Aries again. "I never thought things could get worse than they were in Faerie. I didn't know about the cruelty of humans."

"Is that why you left me that day? The pranks?" Aries asks, and he sounds so genuinely curious, I can't get angry.

"That's the second time you've said that," I murmur. He can't be lying, it's not possible. So he at least believes he's telling the truth…which makes no sense.

I think back to that day and the memory comes easily.

"Where is Prince Aodhan?" I ask, and even in memory my voice is weak.

Anik laughs and the sound is the same as the one that startled me a moment before. "How perfectly naive. The auf actually thinks the prince cares for him." He pins me with his gaze, much like Prince Aodhan had done to the poor butterfly when we were children, though he'd used the thorns of a blackberry branch to pierce the flimsy wings.

"He…he said…" I answer, my voice shaking, but I can't get the words out.

He said he loved me. He said we'd run away together. *It's what I meant to say, but in the face of their crooked grins, I can't choke them out. My voice is like thistledown.*

"He…he said," Anwynn mocks. "He said what you needed to hear and nothing more. Whispered sweet nothings and you just couldn't wait to let him pluck your petals."

"That's not true," I whisper, but something in my chest seems to fall. It's not true…right? Prince Aodhan…my prince…he wouldn't do that to me, would he?

Just like he wouldn't turn the meat in your mouth rancid, or twist your hair into elfknots in your sleep, *I think. But he had, hadn't he? So many times he had, only to turn around and smile his sweet smile until I forgive him, then he does it again.*

Had this been another of his pranks? I don't want to believe it. I don't want to think that he could touch me so gently, sink into my body like I was the only cool water on a hot day, and have it mean nothing.

"What worth is a flower whose petals have been plucked? Just a useless stem." Alberich cups his groin in his hand and squeezes it in a vulgar gesture. "If he saw something of value in you, would he not have been here when you awoke? Would he not be here still, whispering sweet nothings in your ear as he braids your hair with ribbon and daisies?"

I flinch, pained by his reminder that I had indeed woken alone. If Prince Aodhan truly loved me as he promised, would he not have treated me as his equal? Even the lowliest faerie, upon gifting their body to another, was rewarded with at least a clover. And I had awoken with nothing.

My shoulders hunch and I pull the sheet higher. "Why are you here?" Even if Prince Aodhan had lied, even if it was a prank, surely he would not have trusted others in his bedroom without him. There's no such thing as trust between faeries, not even ones as close as Anik and Aodhan.

"Now that he's had you, do you think he actually wants to see your face a moment longer? Your stinking human sweat is staining his sheets. We're here to take you away until he's forgotten your...lackluster performance," Anik says, and the other two snicker. They don't even bother to hide their laughter.

The embarrassed heat I'd felt earlier disappears, leaving behind only cold. Lackluster? Last night, Prince Aodhan had only praise to speak, whispering to me how lovely my skin looked in the moonlight, how soft and warm it felt beneath his hands...how tightly my channel had held him.

A sob tears from my throat and I hide my face in my hands, ashamed that I'd believed him. I scramble off the mattress, dragging the sheet with me as I fumble for clothing. The prince's, discarded the night before like my honor.

But Anik kicks the trousers away from me before I can grip them. "Oh, you won't need those. A dog has no use for clothing, and that's all you're good for now. Our little bitch, courtesy of the prince and his good nature." Anik kneels in front of me and smiles, his teeth sharp. "Brothers...I think he's crying."

And to my shame, I was.

"Why wouldn't I? I came back to my home with a crown of orchids to string through your hair and you were gone. My bed was cold, and you were *gone.*" His voice breaks on the last word.

"Of course I was gone!" I answer, practically yelling. "I woke up to an empty bed but not an empty room. Your so-called friends made it clear what little you thought of me. They— I don't want to talk of this." I tug my knees to my chest.

Those memories were some of the first I'd locked away. Having them back...I can't say I'm happy about it.

"What did they tell you?" Aries asks, his voice quiet, strangled.

"That you didn't want to see my face any longer. That my stinking human sweat was staining your sheets and you wanted them to take me away until you forgot my...my lackluster performance." I feel my cheeks burn. "That you gave me to them to be their little bitch." This time, it's my voice that breaks.

"I *never* said that. I didn't know they were coming to speak to you. I swear I didn't ask them to." He sounds sincere, and I know he's not lying...but if he's not lying, then I need to look at that memory through a different lens.

If Anik and his shadows were acting on their own, if Aries really hadn't known...then I had been the one to leave.

Had he come back, expecting to find me and finding only an empty bed? Had he felt the same sadness?

"I...I don't believe you!" I blurt, my voice strained...desperate. But I do believe him, because he cannot lie. "I... You *had* to know. I'm not the one who left. I'm *not*." I slam my eyes closed. I can't look at him right now.

Pressure builds in my chest and my heart feels like a sledgehammer against my ribs. I can't breathe—I'm suffocating. I rip the torn fabric off my face to uncover my mouth, gasping in a breath that doesn't help.

I jerk up onto my knees and stare frantically around me. The tent is getting smaller, closing in on me. I want out but the sandstorm is still raging outside it. I feel the way the walls vibrate as the wind buffets them.

Something is keening, a mournful wail that hums in my ears, and I realize it's me. I swallow the sound and it comes out a choked gasp. Inside me, the monster stirs, and my panic grows. Not here, not now...not in this enclosed tent with nowhere to run and nowhere to hide.

I dig my fingernails, already trying to sharpen into claws, into the flesh of my arm, the painful scraping rooting me to the present.

"—ry. Rory..." Aries is talking, his voice coming to me as if through a tunnel. I shake my head but it doesn't mute him. He gets louder, and his hands close around my wrists, holding me in place. At some point, he's yanked off the makeshift mask.

I stare blankly at my red-stained fingers. I don't feel the pain of my shredded skin, just the itch of the wounds sluggishly pulling themselves closed.

"I think perhaps we were both deceived," Aries says, hands still on my skin, and his voice is kind. "I counted them my friends. I thought myself untouchable. I was shortsighted. There are more ways to harm someone than with a blade."

"You thought I left," I say, still caught on that thought like a fish on a hook, the sharp bone digging deeper beneath my skin. I clench and unclench my fists. "I hated you. I hated you *so much* for leaving me, and…" My lips feel brittle. I swipe my tongue over them but it doesn't help. "This whole time, I thought that you knew…knew, and just didn't care."

"Knew?" Aries releases one of my wrists and brushes his fingers over my cheek. He tips my face up, forcing me to meet his eyes. "Knew what, baby?"

"What they were doing to me," I answer, numb now as I turn my thoughts back to that time. The worst of it all had been knowing that Aries *knew* and just…didn't care. And not only didn't care, but had given his permission for it.

How different would that horrid time had been if I'd known? Would I still have fled through the Tear the first chance I got?

I draw in a ragged breath. "After that day, the day we…" I trail off, unable to say the word 'fucked', not when it had always felt, even after, like so much more. "After we coupled, where did you go? I never saw you in the castle."

And I hadn't left the castle for what felt like centuries, though it was impossible to measure time accurately in Faerie in general, let alone under the influence of Salvia.

"I left," Aries answers, so quietly I almost can't hear him over the storm. "I needed time away. I couldn't bear the thought of running into you with someone else. The thought of seeing you, happy without me, after what we shared…" Aries drops his hands from my skin. He tucks them into his lap, loosely curled as if to prevent himself from wringing them.

"I joined the Border Guard. Served a handful of rotations at the Golden Coast fighting off the *Ceirean-cròin* before I grew bored of the food." He grins, though it's a weak smile. "Golden Faeries eat only seal and saltwater. I'm told it's an acquired taste."

The *Ceirean-cròin*, if my faded memory is accurate, were water dragons. Large enough to swallow a whale whole with room left over for a ship or three, and capable of shifting to a shoal of silver fish to lure in the unwary. I shudder at the thought of him hunting one.

"I was at the North Border when the Morrigan rose to power." Aries' faint smile dies immediately. I feel my skin go cold.

Even I, doped and drugged as I had been at the time, had heard of the Morrigan. What was fact and what was rumor, I to this day don't know, but the nightmares still come on occasion. She'd risen quickly through the Unsidhe ranks to become General of their armies.

She was the first Unsidhe General to win a battle on Sidhe soil...and her army had celebrated their victory by gorging their bellies at the Nursery. In one night, they'd swallowed an entire generation.

Even I, who—especially then—hated faeries with the heat of a thousand suns, had mourned.

I shudder at the memory of those days. All the uncertainty and pain at the Sidhe Court had the faeries seeking an outlet for it. I and the other Changelings had suffered more in those days than any before or after.

There were times I feared I wouldn't survive—and many more, I feared I would. Then the Tear opened and I'd taken the chance to step through it. I never heard how the war ended. I knew it had, of course, since the

Sidhe bastards eventually started emigrating to Earth after the Collapse. I'd greased enough palms through the years to know Queen Nuala was still in power and neither court had fallen completely.

The bitch Queen had retained enough sway to convince the humans that the Unsidhe were little better than beasts, keeping them from attaining the same visas her people enjoyed.

"Didn't have much time to wallow then," Aries continues speaking, his voice melancholy. "It was a dark time. Faerie still bears the scars from it." He presses his palm to the hard ground. "She cried for…a long time." He meets my eyes, a sad smile on his lips. "So did I. And…not just for the loss of life. I saw your hair in the sunrise, your eyes in the moss. Your skin in the sand." His smile fades. "Rua —" He swallows and corrects himself. "*Rory.* What did she do to you?"

Chapter Twenty-One

Rory

I know who 'she' is. Queen Nuala was many things, but jealous first and foremost. The only females permitted in the castle were the servants, slaves and Sluts, lesser faeries all of them. Female high fae were forced out to the cities and villages so as not to steal attention the Queen felt belonged solely to her.

I stare at the apex of the tent where the pole holds up the fabric, unable to meet his eyes. "I spent…many, many years trying to forget. I painted the memories into murals and locked them away." I sigh and drop my gaze. "Do you know what happens when you carve out pieces of yourself and bury them? When you know you're scared of the dark and of growing things and the smell of blackberries but you can't remember why?"

My voice breaks and I swallow, my breath ragged. Aries doesn't answer and I don't give him time to. "I have enough nightmares for both of us, Aries. Telling you of that time will not erase the memories, nor will it heal the scars in here." I lift my fingertips to my temple.

"A shared burden is lighter," Aries argues, and he reaches across the space between us to take my hands. His skin is warm against mine.

I fight the urge to yank mine away. Touching him feels good…too good. And good things rarely last, in my experience. Instead, I squeeze his hands, holding on like a lifeline.

"Or it drags us both down instead. I do not need you to punish yourself with the knowledge of something you did not cause and could not have changed." Gathering my courage, I scooch along the hard dirt to sit at his side, still clutching his hand. "Instead, could we put the past where it belongs? Soon enough, we will be forced to separate again. I'd rather spend these last few days getting to know you again."

Aries looks like he wishes to argue but instead, he nods. Then, he smiles and lets go of my hands. Before I can mourn the loss, he holds out his right one. "Good afternoon, fair stranger. I am called Aries."

I take his hand in mine and shake it. "I am called Rory. It is a pleasure to make your acquaintance."

Suddenly feeling playful, I shift up to my knees and give him a coy smile. I know he had no plans of holding me to the old rules of sanctuary, not unless…not unless I make him. Once I speak the words, his faerie nature won't allow him not to act.

Maybe it's crazy…but they didn't call me Raving Rory for nothing.

I need to see this side of him. More than that, I need to know that I can still do this. I need to prove to myself that Faerie hasn't broken me.

"Kind stranger," I say, proud that my voice only shakes a little. "I beg shelter from the storm. Have you room for a poor orphan boy in your tent?"

Aries grins, sudden and bright. It is an old ritual and I can feel the magic between us, the beginnings of the contract stirring to life. "Silly human. Don't you know the dangers of seeking shelter from a faerie?"

He's giving me an out.

I don't take it. "Whatever do you mean, good sir?"

Aries doesn't speak for several long seconds that draw out between us, precarious as a tight rope.

"You may weather the storm in my tent for the price of a dance," Aries says, and the ritual words seem to echo.

Outside, the wind thunders.

Inside, my heart pounds.

I shouldn't want this, to dance for him. Part of me doesn't — the part that remembers dancing for faeries until my feet bled, skin flayed from muscles and stripped back to expose bone.

But a larger part of me *needs* this, to dance for him by *my* choice.

"I accept," I say, my voice breathless. The contract snaps in place, invisible binds wrapping around my wrists and ankles. I stand slowly, my head brushing the fabric of the tent. Tension is tight in my spine but my neck is straight and proud.

Aries sits, still as stone, with his eyes on my body. His gaze is hot as fire. I feel it kissing my skin.

"Tell me, kind stranger..." I pause, grinning suddenly. His breath is bated. Mine is not. I'm sure of what he expects. The old me, the me he knew before I grew old and jaded, would have been sweet about it, shy.

I'm not that boy anymore. "Have you ever been to a strip club?"

Aries' eyes widen and his mouth parts. I hear, even over the wind, the sharp breath he sucks in.

I grin. "Oh, you *have*. You naughty boy." I step almost to the center of the tent, beside the flimsy pole keeping the ceiling from collapsing down on us. I won't be able to move as much as I'd like, not with the slope of the tent roof and the tight quarters, and I can't use the pole the way I wish to, but I've danced in worse conditions.

I start to sway my hips to music only I can hear. I press my palm to my belly — ignoring the way it feels sunken. I cannot think of the weight I've lost and the effects my time in Faerie has had on my body, not if I want to do this right. It's hard to feel sexy with every rib on display.

I drag my hand up, lifting my shirt along with it to flash Aries a glimpse of bare skin before it falls again. I let my hand trail over my chest slowly until I reach my neck, then tangle my fingers in my hair, mussing it up.

I've seen the way he watches me. I know what parts of my body he can't help but look at and my hair is at the top of the list. There was a time when all I wanted to do was cut it off. Now, I use it to tease him.

It's working. He swallows, his Adam's apple bobbing in his throat, and his eyes are fixed on me. I can't raise my arms above my head the way I'd like, not without taking the tent down around us, but I make do.

I skim my fingers over my lips instead, drawing his gaze to them so I can blow him a kiss, then drop my hands to the hem of my shirt again. This time, I grip the fabric and slowly pull it over my head. I let it fall somewhere behind me.

The air around us is hot and thick with arousal. My pink nipples perk up and I tweak them, one after another, before cupping them demurely in my palms. A flutter of my eyelashes and he's eating out of my hand. I can see the bulge tenting his pants.

I continue to sway as I step a bit closer. "Help me with the button?" I ask, my voice breathy as I angle my hips toward him.

Aries' hands are shaking as he fumbles with it. If I didn't know better, I'd say he's as nervous as a virgin. I smirk down at him. "Feeling shy, Highness?"

He swallows but sets his jaw. His eyes are fire as he grips my pants and tugs them down. It's not the tease I planned on, but I can't say I'm disappointed to step out of the bunched fabric. He throws them to the side. They smack into the tent but neither of us bother watching them land. Instead, I watch the hunger in his eyes and he watches the dance my dick is doing.

It twitches under his gaze. I feel the sticky pre-cum already leaking.

Aries and I have had many problems in the past…but arousal was never one of them. He turns me on like no other ever has. He lifts his hand toward my thigh and I step back, *tsking*. "Now, now, Highness. No touching the dancers."

I wait, breath bated, to see what he'll do. Will he ignore me, touch my flesh like he owns it anyway? Every inch of me is his and always have been. Sometimes, I hate it, the way my body has given itself to him with little input from me.

Or will he submit? Curl his fine-boned hands into fists in his laps and watch me with that hunger — a man starving for my body, with only me to decide if I feed it to him?

I can't decide which option I prefer.

He does neither. Instead, he leans back and stretches his legs out, one on either side of me, and shoves his hand into the waistband of his pants. He fishes out his dick, the skin darker at the root but lightening to a delicious pink near the crown.

He gives himself a smooth stroke and smirks. "Then I'll have to touch myself, won't I?"

I'm not jealous of his hand. I'm *not.*

I retaliate by gripping my own dick in a firm grasp. "Are you sure your hand is where you want to spill?"

"Do I have a better offer?" Aries asks, lifting his brow but not slowing his strokes. I lick my lips as a bead of clear fluid forms on his slit.

"Be a...a good boy," I stutter, unused to taking a dominant role. It feels foreign. I want nothing more than to let him take control but fear grows stones in my throat at the thought. I'm not ready yet. I've had too many faeries hold me down and fuck me up. I want to taste him, but I'm not ready yet for more than that. So instead of giving him my ass, I say, "and I'll let you fuck my mouth."

His hand stills on his cock and he appears to think. He leans back, his free hand propping him up. "I don't know...you said I couldn't touch the dancers."

I give a provocative shake of my hips, then spin slowly to give him a good view of my firm ass. I don't think I'm imagining the way he groans. Once I'm facing him again, I say, "You don't need to touch my skin to shove your dick down my throat, do you?"

The skin of his knuckles tightens as he grips his cock hard enough that I know it has to hurt.

"I...I can be good," Aries grits out between clenched teeth.

I laugh. "Something tells me it doesn't come naturally to you, does it?" I don't give him time to answer. Instead, I step closer and drop to my knees in front of him. "Stand up, Highness, and put your hands behind your back. If you touch me, I stop."

"Okay, sunshine," he murmurs, and his eyes soften. I suspect he knows why I can't let him touch me now. I flinch, then curse myself for showing weakness. He stands slowly, careful not to even brush against my skin, and fists his hands behind his back. I lean forward to take his dick in my mouth but he steps back.

Confused, I meet his gaze. His expression is serious as he stares down at me. "I accept your dance as payment for a night of sanctuary," he says, and I feel the magic of the contract fade away. "This is not a bargain, Rory," he explains, tipping his chin toward his erection. "I don't expect you to do anything you don't wish to. You can stop at any point."

I feel myself flush. On the one hand, I appreciate that he clarified. I hadn't thought of it as part of my dance, but without the spoken words, Faerie might have. If I'd stopped partway through, who knows whether the land would have considered it a bargain broken.

On the other hand, I hate that he sees my fear and felt the need for clarification in the first place.

"I understand," I mumble, then swallow his dick in one try. I don't want him to draw me into an explanation or discussion—don't want to risk him thinking me too broken to enjoy this.

Maybe I am, because for the first few seconds, I panic at the weight of him on my tongue, the way his shaft prods insistently at the back of my throat until I gag. After the initial panic, though, his taste helps root me in the moment. It is nothing like the others.

They had all tasted of mint—overpowered by the Salvia plant fogging my thoughts.

Aries is sweet, all honey and sugar.

The difference is enough to ground me here, in the moment.

Aries groans. "Fuck," he curses, and even with his dick in my mouth I can see how his abs clench and his shoulders twitch like he's barely restraining himself from grabbing me.

I feel a rush of power. I'm not the same weak boy I used to be. I know he could take control in a heartbeat if he wished. I'm surprised to realize that I trust that he won't. Trust…something I never thought I'd feel again, least of all in *Aries.*

It's a liberating feeling. For the first time in a long time, I'm not angry or scared.

I'm free.

Prince Aries

Gods, his mouth is heaven. The tight, wet heat of his mouth, the emerald fire burning in his eyes…even the scratch of his nails against my thighs when he grips my legs. My knees go weak and I clench my hands tighter to avoid sinking them into his tresses.

"Fuck, sweetheart…I'm close already," I groan. "You…you have to pull off— Fuck!" I curse again as he swirls his tongue along the underside of my crown, a particularly sensitive spot.

He doesn't stop. He sucks harder. His own dick is hard as stone, untouched between his legs. Pleasure courses through my body like lightning. I unclench my hands jerk them up to my head instead. My scalp is covered in scratchy stubble. I curl my fingers against my skin, doing whatever I can to avoid acting on instinct and grabbing him.

I don't know what happened to him at my mother's hands—I'm not sure I want to know, either—but I can guess. From the way he flinched and the fear in his eyes earlier, to the way he told me to keep my hands to myself, I know my suspicions are right.

"Rory, it's not safe. You c-can't—" I start to stutter.

He pulls off, curling his fingers around my shaft and squeezing. "It's safe. I want to taste you, Aries. You won't hurt me."

He says it with such conviction that I want to believe him but I'm afraid to. I've lost too many friends, too many lovers…my erection threatens to wilt despite his hand stroking me.

"I can't lose you now. I feel like I just found you…" I say, and I don't realize that I'm shaking until Rory's face softens. The image of dead lovers from my past tries to overlay over his but I don't let them. They aren't here, Rory is.

"You won't lose me, not from this," Rory promises, but he doesn't take me in his mouth again. Once I realize that, my fear wanes and I can concentrate on the feeling of his fingers stroking my shaft again. It's a different sort of pleasure than his mouth was but it doesn't take him long to bring me back to the edge again.

"Almost there," I stutter, breath coming faster.

He angles the head of my dick toward his chest and that's enough to tip me over the edge. With a gasp, I spill over the edge. My climax paints his chest with streaks of sticky white.

My knees go weak and I sink down on my ass. I can't take my eyes off him. That's my cum on his skin, my scent marking him as *mine.* I've never felt this possessive before. Rory is special. Rory is *mine.*

I watch as he sits back on his ass. He slides his hand through my seed, coating his palm with my spend. Then, he cups his dick and starts to stroke, fast and careless, using my cum as lube. The crown of his cock is an angry red and in seconds, he's brought himself off. His own seed stains the chapped dirt.

I feel jealous of Faerie as she tastes it.

Faerie feels far too pleased beneath us.

Chapter Twenty-Two

Rory

Outside, the wind still howls, but inside the tent is silent. I stare at Aries. He stares at me. My breath, ragged from the strength of my orgasm, starts to slow. Now that the pleasure is fading, the air between us feels stale and awkward.

Our mutual orgasms did little to change the history between us. Our relationship, if it could be called that, was strained by more than just a miscommunication.

He may not have sent his friends to drag me from his bed, and I may not have left as willingly as he'd assumed, but the very fact we'd been eager to believe the worst about each other proves our relationship's fragility. It will take more than an orgasm to mend it, if we even want to.

I'm fleeing to the Unsidhe for safety and Aries...I don't know what his plans are. Go back to being the obedient prince at his mother's knee? Return to Earth once he knows I'm safe?

My shoulders hunch at the thought.

"What do —" I start to ask his plans but he speaks at the same time. "I don't want —"

We both go silent. It stretches awkwardly between us and Aries breaks it first. He draws in a breath. "I don't want to lose you," he admits. "Not when I feel like I've just got you back."

"I can't stay here," I answer, voice little more than a whisper. I don't want to lose him either, but what choice do we have? The Unsidhe won't grant him sanctuary. They'd be crazy too...he is his mother's child. They would not trust him...how could they? And I can't stay. Queen Nuala would not allow me to sit at her son's side, not when she has made it clear that the only place for a mortal in Faerie is beneath her feet.

"Will you come back to me? If my mother was no longer a threat...would you return?" Aries asks, his voice pleading.

I open my mouth to reply but force myself to wait, to think of his question and answer it honestly. "I don't know," I admit. "I want to explore this...whatever this is...that we have between us." I press my hand to his chest. His skin is warm and soft, hairless as many of the fae are. "But I'm scared."

Aries looks pained. "I understand. My kind...and I myself" — he looks reluctant to admit — "have not been kind to you or yours. You have the right to your fear. I will not begrudge you that."

"I don't *want* to be scared," I say, hating how sullen my voice comes out. Childish, when I have not been a child in many, many years.

"We all want things that we cannot have," Aries replies, and there is a weight to his words. A weight that speaks of experience and loss.

I sigh. Now that the heat of the moment has passed, his spend on my skin is only itchy and I long to pull on my pants to hide my sticky, flaccid cock. But at the same time, the air is still hot and my skin is slippery with sweat. I drag them on anyway, unwilling to sit my bare ass on the cracked dirt. I do leave off my shirt, though.

Aries, who never fully stripped, just hikes his pants up and re-buttons them. We sit together but miles apart in our own minds.

Outside, the storm continues to rage.

Sometime later — it's hard to know how long without the sun to gauge time with — I crawl over to the tent flap.

"Do you think it's night yet?" I ask, trying to see out the very small slit between two of the ties. It looks dark — but the sandstorm had blocked the light of the suns so well, that's not a change.

"Got a hot date?" Aries asks, voice droll. He's lying on his back, legs bent at the knees to make room for his tall frame. One arm is over his eyes, the other pillowing his head.

I sigh and drop back onto the ground across from him. There's nothing to look at except the vibrating brown fabric of the tent. "How much longer do you think this will last?"

"Hard to say," Aries replies. He doesn't sound concerned. In fact, he sounds like he's half asleep.

"What if we run out of water?" I ask. My lips feel chapped and my mouth is full of invisible cotton. My waterskin is nearly empty.

"It is a possibility," Aries says. "But I'm more concerned the tent pole won't hold up and the sand will bury us alive."

"How reassuring," I mutter, turning my eyes to the admittedly flimsy wood. A crack runs jagged down the side of it.

"Don't worry so much. Faerie won't let us die," Aries says.

"Maybe won't let *you* die. I somehow doubt Faerie cares much about me." Huffing, I go back to staring at the sloped ceiling of the tent. Below me, the ground rumbles.

After a second, Aries says, "Faerie says you're too amusing to let die so easy. She called up the storm to throw our pursuers off our tracks. It will settle by second dawn."

"Any idea how long until then?" I roll my head to the side to stare at him. He looks far too comfortable over there, like he's on a feather-down mattress. Beneath me, a dozen stones are jabbing into my back.

"It will come when it comes," Aries answers, shrugging.

"Fuck this," I curse to myself and roll to my knees, crawling around the tent pole to his side of the tent.

"Oof!" he groans as I clamber onto him.

"You're softer than the dirt," I explain as I try to make myself comfortable.

"That's not a compliment," Aries wheezes. He doesn't try to shove me off though.

"Oh, whatever," I grumble, dropping my head onto his chest. He's not much bigger than me and honestly, not much softer than the ground. His muscles might as well be rocks.

I can't make myself move though. I want to be close to him while I can. In a few days, he'll be gone out of my life again and I don't want to dwell on that now. I shift again and he grunts as my elbow accidentally sinks into his stomach.

"Shh," I say, patting his shoulder. "Mattresses don't talk."

I must fall asleep at some point.

"Whatever you'll let me." Aries' voice is honey sweet. I don't know if I should trust him, but I want to. He's been nice lately. Maybe too nice. Maybe this is another prank. It would be better — for me and my sanity — to act like it is. Aries is the only person in this whole world who has the power to truly hurt me. Certainly others could break my body, rend my skin or snap my bones, but my heart would be safe.

When I was smaller, I'd thought my life would be a fairy tale. Aries, the other half of my soul, would open his eyes and see me, truly see me, and everything would be fine. Then I grew up. The flutter like butterfly wings in my chest makes me fear that I haven't grown up — or out of my silly infatuation that no amount of mischief by him had managed to kill — as much as I'd thought.

"I'll let you do just about anything," I admit. My heart is pounding. Am I making a mistake? Maybe. Will I regret this tomorrow morning?

No. I don't think I will. Even if this all falls apart...even if he stabs me in my naked back in the morning, I can't pass up this chance to have him.

It might be the only chance I get.

He takes my hand. His is larger than mine and his skin several shades darker. "Your glamour..." I start to ask, then swallow, hesitant.

His hand tightens on mine. "What about it?" he asks, and his voice has an edge of ice to it. I was going to ask if he would drop it. He rarely let anyone see his true self, with his willowy body and youthful face. I couldn't remember the last time I'd seen it.

"Nothing," I say, changing my mind.

He hums but doesn't comment. Instead, he loosens his grip on my hand and turns, leading me down the path through the woods toward his cottage. I'm familiar with it, of course. I'd spent most of my life sleeping on the floor at the foot of his bed. It was only recently that the bond between our souls had grown strong enough – or Aries himself had – that we could spend nights apart from each other. Sure, we'd taken the odd night or two away but longer than that and our bond would start to burn.

The prince's cottage is tucked inside the castle walls but separate from the castle itself. It is made of cobbled stone of varying colors. The door is living wood and each of the two windows are composed of carefully pieced together crystal. Opaque enough to not be able to see through from the outside but clear enough to let in light. It is nothing like the elaborate castle his Queen-mother lives in and some days, I suspect that's exactly why he chose it. He could have lived anywhere and he chose this.

Aries runs his free hand over the soft bark on the door and it quivers open. The inside is almost exactly how I remember. A large bed of moss against the far wall with golden, spider-silk sheets and a headboard made of elegantly carved racks of elk antlers. He has a banked fire in the hearth, an empty pipkin set on the stones off to the side.

From the look of it, he hasn't used it since I was here the last time – though for a very different reason. At least, I hope so. If he coerces me into cleaning his chamber pot and cooking him breakfast instead of relieving me of my virginity, I might scream.

The door closes. For a second, I feel its presence behind me. I've never cared about the spirit of the tree lingering in the cottage before...but I've never planned to participate in unspeakable things in here before either.

I swallow around the sudden lump in my throat as Aries faces me, releasing my hand to cup my face instead. His skin is hot on mine...or maybe the heat is mine. Nerves make it hard to breathe. I want this, but I'm afraid. Afraid it will hurt, or I won't like it. Afraid I'll disappoint him.

Mostly the latter.

"Don't be scared," Aries murmurs. He's always been able to read me so well. "I'll take care of you."

"I've never done this," I say, embarrassed to admit it. Aries is as far from a virgin as anyone could get. I've witnessed him tumble many a lover in any number of places, from the castle gardens to the wildflower meadows to the banks of the fast-rushing stream in the forest. He wasn't shy. Most faeries weren't.

Aries brushes my lower lip with his thumb, tugging on it gently until my mouth parts on a gasp. "So pretty," Aries murmurs. "Hard to believe I'll be the first to taste you."

Chapter Twenty-Three

Rory

I wake up suddenly, heart pounding, to a silent tent. The only sound is the blood rushing through my ears. My chest feels tight with fear, though of what I'm not sure. Certainly not from my dreams. The air is surprisingly chilly, drawing up goosebumps on my arms. Slowly, I crack open my eyes.

Everything is as I expect it to be. Aries' bag is by the side of the tent, the pole is cracked but still standing strong. My shirt is crumpled on the dirt. And beneath me is Aries, breath slow with sleep.

There's nothing to explain what woke me, or my fear. Then, I realize that the quiet I hear means the storm is over.

"Aries," I hiss, shaking his shoulder as I sit up. He wakes with a start. "It's over."

He blinks his eyes owlishly at me before realization fills them. "We should get moving. It's going to be a long, hot walk. We need to reach water soon."

I scramble off him and grab my shirt, yanking it over my head.

"Wait," Aries says, urging me to sit. "I have an idea." He takes the shirt he'd ripped yesterday and starts to tie the shredded fabric around my feet. "They won't protect you from the stones, but they should help with the heat."

"What, tired of carrying me already?" I ask with a grin, though I'm inwardly grateful.

"Never," Aries answers, but his face is sober. "If Faerie thought we were being followed close enough to warrant a sandstorm, I have to expect they could catch up with us still. I want you to be able to run if you need to." He meets my eyes. "And if you need to run, then I trust you to do it. They aren't here for me, so don't play the hero."

"You want me to leave you," I clarify, numb at the thought.

"I want you to keep yourself safe. They won't harm me, but if I have to worry about you, they might get lucky," he answers. I know he's right, but I hate it. I hate the thought of leaving him behind even more than the thought of being out here on my own.

"Promise me," he urges, hands clasping my ankles.

"If it comes to that…" I swallow, the words getting stuck in my throat. I clear it then try again. "I promise I will consider it."

His grip tightens for a second and he clenches his jaw, but he gives me a curt nod of understanding. I will not make a promise that I'm not sure I can keep, not here on Faerie soil.

Quickly, we work open the ties and dig our way through the mounded sand to emerge into the chilly morning. I start to sink into the soft powder and panic for a moment, fearing it will swallow me whole. Fortunately, it's been packed down tight a few feet down and I'm able to get my footing. Grains of sand cling to my skin as I straighten.

It takes several tense minutes to move enough sand from the sides for us to reach the stakes but everything after that is easy. We do it together in near silence. We break down the tent together in near silence. Aries shoves the disassembled pieces back into his bag before he slips it over his shoulder. I scan the horizon for any sign of movement. I see nothing, but I can't shake the feeling that we're being watched.

"Good thing we have a map," I mutter as I turn back to Aries. "Everything looks the same now." The cracked dirt and strewn rocks have all been blanketed by a soft covering of scarlet sand. There are no landmarks to gauge distance, no footsteps to show where we've come from. Even the pit where the tent had rested is already being hidden by the shifting red powder.

"It would be too easy to get lost out here, doomed to wander for eternity," Aries says, face sober. For the first time in a long while, I see the difference between who he is now and who he used to be. This is the man who joined the Bureau of Arcane Ability — who investigated crimes and consoled victims and lived to serve and protect. He is not the same mischief-loving prankster of my memories.

"I bet you were a good agent," I say, seemingly off the cuff if his surprised look is anything to go by. "I couldn't see it yesterday," I elaborate. "I thought I knew who you were. A spoiled prince with no tact and a complete inability to be serious or sensitive." I smile in an attempt to soften the words. "But you've changed. I'm the one who's stuck in the past."

Aries' face gentles. "I doubt you've had a chance to do anything but survive."

I flush and avert my gaze. "We should get going. Um…" I fumble the quiver around so I can stretch my hand into it and pull out the map. Unfurling it, I spend a few extra seconds staring to regain my composure. I hate that he's right...I *haven't* done anything but struggle to survive.

First through the Queen's torture, then on the streets of a world I didn't understand. My body might have been born on Earth but I had no memories of it when I returned. I'd learned enough to survive — that not all food was safe to eat, especially if you were pulling it out of the big green metal containers called 'dumpsters', that people who said they lost their dog often didn't have a dog, and nothing good ever happened in a dark alley.

I'd never quite figured out currency, which is why I always preferred pinching shiny things instead of cash. I could take the rings and necklaces and fancy silverware to the man on the corner — I didn't ask his name and he didn't ask mine — and he'd give me food in glass jars with tight metal rings for lids, bags of fruit or fresh picked vegetables, and large gallons of clean water, unfortunately stored in nasty plastic jugs. Sometimes, he'd even throw in a few new sets of clothing when mine were particularly ragged.

I'd gotten my favorite pair of chunky black lace-up boots from him. He said he'd taken them off the body of a homeless man, but I suspected whoever they'd come from had died from a more...violent death. I didn't ask what the man on the corner did for work when he wasn't hawking stolen goods and he didn't tell. I already knew the answer — the tattoo of an eye on his neck was distinctive. He was a member of the local gang, the Watchers.

I must have been standing here staring at the map, unseeing, for longer than I realize, because Aries takes it gently from my hands to look it over himself. "We need to go North by Northeast another fifteen klicks, then head...I'd estimate another five clicks to reach the Dead Woods." I can hear him capitalize the title in his head, even though they weren't on the map. "They don't look very thick...if we're lucky, we could be on the shores of the loch by nightfall."

"When are we ever lucky?" I say dryly.

Aries' lips twitch but he doesn't laugh. Instead, he says, "Try not to jinx us, brat."

I can't resist sticking out my tongue but it lightens the mood between us enough that I'm able to concentrate on the here and now. I hold my hand out for the map. Aries only hesitates a moment before rolls it up and passes it over. I tuck it safely into the quiver, which I let hang over my shoulder against my back again.

"Well, what are we waiting for?" Grinning, feeling lighter than I have in days, I push past him and start the trek. His laugh is quiet as he follows. The torn-up shirt around my feet is helping with the heat, though this early in the day, the sun has barely started to kiss the sand. By first noon, I doubt it'll be much protection, especially since I sink down a good few inches with every step. The grains of sand stick to my ankles and the lower stretch of my calves, easily getting under the hem of my pant legs.

The walk isn't terrible at first. The ground isn't as hard, thanks to the sand dumped by the storm, and the air is dry but not sweltering. As the two suns creep higher in the sky, it starts to get hotter by the second. Soon, sweat is pooling in my pits and at the small of my back, chafing my inner legs, and I start to reevaluate my comfort level.

The worst is the silence. Even our footsteps are muffled. There are no birds, no camels, no snakes…no wind. And everywhere I look is the same. No rocks casting shadows, no cacti or plants, just a seemingly endless stretch of deep red sand. Without the suns to gauge direction—always, no matter the season, they rise from the North—it would be too easy to get lost and wander forever.

Walking into the sun gets old quickly. My eyes are watering and I find myself wishing for sunglasses. Many things from Earth seemed pointless, like junk food that had no nutritional value, fashion magazines—who thought wearing live crickets sewn into the linings of their jackets was attractive? The chirping had to be annoying, not to mention the fact that eventually, you would be walking around with dead bugs in your clothes—but right now, I'd kill for pair of Abalone true-black shades, or a large floppy rimmed hat.

My feet are on fire—not literally, but it feels like it— well before first noon, and by second my skin has that tight feeling promising a sunburn later. With my luck, I'll blister worse than a plague victim.

Aries, of course, is glowing.

And with his knee-high boots, not even bothered by the sand.

Fucker.

Aries

It's been a long time since I've enjoyed heat like this. Having been stationed at headquarters in Old York, most of my cases kept me around the Northeastern states. Sometimes, I'd end up as far south as North Carolina or as far west as Nebraska, but it was rare. There was enough crime in the state of York to keep the entire field office up to their ears in cases without having to look elsewhere. Summers were short and far from sweet—a sticky heat and more thunderstorms than clear skies.

I tip my face back and close my eyes for a second. I'm not worried about tripping—out here in the sand, there's nothing to trip *on* – and as quiet as it is, I trust that I will hear anything we need to worry about long before it becomes an issue.

I take a second to breathe in the dry desert air. The heat seems to melt away the remaining tension clinging to my body, leaving me more relaxed than I've felt in ages. I suspect the feeling comes at least in part because I know Rory is beside me, safe.

It's hitting me now, I think for the first time. Rory is here, alive. He didn't die all those years ago after leaving Faerie, or at my mother's hands. He's alive. I didn't realize what a heavy weight his disappearance had left on my shoulders until it was gone.

I hear the sound of his slap before I feel the sting on my arm. "What?" I ask, startled, rubbing my arm as I turn to stare at him in surprise.

"You look far too happy right now," he grumbles. His skin is almost as red as his hair, which looks stringy and limp. The heat is not being kind to him.

"And you look like a mess," I joke, reaching over to tweak his hair. "Don't worry," I say, interrupting whatever he's opened his mouth to say, "it looks good on you."

"I don't care if it looks good on me," Rory protests. "It fucking sucks and it's totally not fair!"

"That's life, sweetheart. You look cute. But here —" I unhook my waterskin from my belt. It's nearly empty. The sandstorm yesterday had put us behind, but even if I'd been able to plan for it, it wouldn't have mattered. We'd filled the skins as full as we could have. "Drink. We're nearly there." *Give or take a few kliks.* Something told me — and that something was the flush in his cheeks and the drying sweat along his hairline — that he needs to hydrate more than I do.

He looks like he wants to argue but thankfully, he bites his tongue and takes the waterskin. I watch, mesmerized, as his lips seem to caress the mouth, his throat shifting with each swallow.

I shouldn't be getting hard now but my dick is a steel rod in my pants. I readjust myself, feeling like a naughty teenager when his eyes catch the motion. His eyes crinkle as he drains the waterskin and hands it back. "Having issues there, Highness?"

"Nothing I can't handle," I reply.

He smirks, teeth biting into his pink lower lip. "I'm sure you can," he murmurs.

"Funny boy," I say rather than show him how well I could handle myself. It's not the place or time. Instead, I hook the empty waterskin back to my belt. He just grins, not bothering to answer.

I didn't need one anyway.

My humor fades as the day goes on and Rory keeps wilting. When he starts to stumble, my worry grows. "Fuck this," I mutter and scoop him up, ignoring his yelp and token protests. "You can barely walk straight, Rory. You need a break, whether you accept it or not."

"You could have *asked*," Rory says but there's no bite to the words. He's more tired than I realized.

"Would you have said yes?" I counter.

He is quiet for several long seconds.

"That's what I thought." I must sound too smug because Rory smacks the back of his hand into my chest. It's weak and that more than anything concerns me. I scan the horizon. I see a dark smudge in the right direction...I have to hope it's the Dead Woods and not a mirage.

"Um...Aries?" Rory says, his voice strained. His eyes are fixed on something behind me. A sense of dread fills me as I turn to look.

A red cloud is moving fast. Someone is following us and they are approaching quickly. One, maybe two people on horseback. Likely no more than that or the cloud would be larger, but in Rory's condition, even one or two could be deadly with a bit of bad luck.

We're too far from the woods to make it before they reach us and even if we did, by the name alone I suspect it won't provide much shelter. I'll need a different plan...and the only one I can think of, I know Rory won't like.

Fuck, I don't like it either. The thought of sending him off on his own threatens to break me out in hives. But we're running out of time. "Listen to me," I say urgently as I lower Rory to his feet. "I need you—no, don't argue," I say when he tries to interrupt me. "We don't have time. I need you to go ahead, as fast as you can. Get to the Dead Woods and find a place to hide. If I'm not there by dusk, you go ahead without me."

"I'm not just going to leave you here," he protests, voice hot with anger.

"You don't have a choice. I can't lose you, Rory. Not when I just got you back. And I can't do what I need to do here if I'm worried about protecting you. One slip up and they'll have us both," I say, pleading that he will listen. The cloud of dust is getting closer as we speak.

"I have a sword. I can help," Rory argues.

I give him a shove, not hard but forceful enough that he stumbles back. "You can barely stand. That sword may be sharp, but you aren't trained to use it," I hazard a guess. After all, swords went out of fashion on Earth before either of us stepped through the Tear. Unless he took a fencing class for fun—doubtful, considering where he was living when I saw him—the closest he's come to using a sword were the times I'd forced him to clean mine all those years ago.

His face goes even redder but he finally nods. "Fine, but you *better* come find me. I'm not done being angry with you and if you let them beat you, I'll feel too sorry for you to be angry, got it?"

"Got it," I agree, watching as he backs away, distress on his face. With a cry, he finally turns and takes off at an unstable run. He's not moving fast. I'll just have to hope he's moving fast enough. I turn my back on his receding form, watching the cloud of dust instead.

I unsheathe *Teremor*, my old friend. She sings an eager cry for battle.

Chapter Twenty-Four

Aries

I recognize the horses before I recognize the faeries astride them. The big roan is Zephyr. His sire was my father's favorite steed. Sixteen hands high, he is still dwarfed by the perlino in the lead. Orchid is my mother's pride and joy, the jewel of her stables. Only one other faerie is allowed astride her.

Anik, my oldest friend. We've exchanged courtesy letters in the years since I left Faerie, enough that I know he goes by Marik now. He's kept my mother's interest for longer than any of her other lovers have managed. Even from this rapidly shrinking distance, I can see he looks good. Better than I would expect, anyway.

My mother's past lovers looked wan and strung out in as little as weeks. He's been fucking her for much, *much* longer.

His expression is solemn. Several yards from me, he brushes his hand lightly over Orchid's neck and the horse slows abruptly, coming to a stop a scant few feet away. The horse tosses her head. Though others might think it makes me look weak, I step back and to the side. One solid kick from the mare and she'd cave in my chest with her dinner-plate hooves.

I am no longer the same appearance-obsessed boy I used to be. The old me thought winning didn't matter unless I did in in style. My years in the Bureau taught me that it's better to survive by fighting ugly than die with flair. Arteria would be proud. He'd spent many long days trying to beat the pride out of me.

"Hail Prince Aries, he who wears the Circlet of the Woodland Hart," Marik greets, tipping his head in respect. "It's been a long time, friend."

"It has," I agree. "I didn't expect to run into you all the way out here." I turn my eyes to the male on the roan. I don't recognize him. His hair is long and dark, his pale face pinched. "Who's your little friend?"

"Hm-mm?" Marik turns his eyes to his partner and his face clears. "Oh, yes. You wouldn't have met. He was blossomed a few years after you left. This is Seronel, my squire."

"Squire? You?" I snort, amused at the thought. The humor doesn't make me sheathe my sword, however. "Since when do you have a squire?"

"Since Arteria passed," Marik answers and I sober up, amusement dying.

"When?" I ask, the first of a dozen questions I now have. When, how…why.

"Not long after you left. There was a skirmish near the border. He led a few squads out to head them off. It was supposed to be an easy fight. Three trolls, that's what the intel said. They were just the decoy. You'll be comforted to know that he died honorably," Marik says, voice soft. Of all of Arteria's apprentices, it was well known that I'd been his favorite, just as he'd been my favorite teacher. In many ways, he'd been like a father to me.

Knowing he died honorably was not as much of a comfort as Marik believes it to be. He'd been a great faerie. The world was worse off for his loss.

"Why did you not write to me?" I ask, throat tight.

"Your mother's orders," Marik answers.

"That doesn't make any sense. She's been fighting for me to return for years. If she'd told me…I would have come home for the Planting." Like many humans on Earth, we faeries bury our dead in the ground. Unlike the humans, we also bury our dead with a seedling.

"You know she's always been jealous of your…relationship with Arteria," Marik says, and it is explanation enough. Mother wanted me back but on her terms. She probably found it amusing to deny me the opportunity to offer my final condolences.

Emotion swells in my chest, a mixture of sadness and pain that swirls like a whirlpool. If I'm not careful, I could drown in it. I shove the feelings down and tighten my grip on the hilt of my sword.

"What are you doing out this way, Marik?" I ask.

"I think you know, Prince Aries. The Queen has ordered the return of the missing changeling. Seronel here is the Queen's best tracker. We thought we lost him during the sandstorm," Marik answers.

"I do not wish to fight you, friend, but I will not let you take him. He is under my protection." I stand straighter. I truly do not wish to fight him, but for Rory I will rend his flesh from his bones if that's what it takes.

"I feared you would say that." Marik sighs and draws his sword. It is not his favored weapon—Rory might have thought I didn't recognize the pommel of the sword at his waist, but I'd just chosen not to mention it. I hadn't wanted to know how he'd stolen my friend's blade.

"New sword?" I ask, stalling.

"It seems someone has borrowed my dear *Odelia*. But fear not, Prince. I am just as capable with *Claudia*." He holds it out slightly for me to examine, but not close enough to risk me potentially disarming him. The blade is rippled and blue, the edges sharp as a razor's edge.

"One of Alric's," I say, and it's not a question. I'd recognize the signature color of the metal anywhere.

"Almost as fine a piece as your beauty," he answers, nodding toward my sword.

"His crowning achievement, in his words," I agree. I'm stalling, we both are. We've fought before but never like this. Never for real. Some of our bouts had been violent but neither one of us had ever crossed the final line.

Marik watches me with eyes older than his years. "You have always been my friend," he says quietly, the same emotion I'm feeling—regret, worry and premature mourning—sounding in his voice.

"Is that why you convinced Ruari that I asked you to take him away that morning? Because you were my friend?" I don't mean for the anger to be so obvious in my voice but now that I know what he did, I find it harder to stay calm seeing him face to face.

Marik's skin pales but he sets his jaw. "I cannot disobey the Queen's orders."

"It was my mother's idea?"

"You had to know what she'd think, Aries. You and a changeling? The Court would never accept it," Marik explains but it doesn't make me feel any better.

"Why would I care what the Court would or wouldn't accept?" Now I'm even more confused. I'd thought perhaps Marik had been playing a poorly thought-out prank, or acting out of a place of jealousy. I'd been spending more time with Ruari those days before that final one, and curtailing many of Marik's attempts at making mischief.

"You are our prince, Aries. When your mother fades, you will take the throne." Marik sounds exasperated, like he's telling me something that should be obvious.

"Yeah, someday in the next ten thousand years or so." I roll my eyes, regretting it immediately. It would have been the perfect opportunity for him to attack but for some reason, his sword stays still.

"No. Sometime in the next one, maybe. Could be less. She—" Marik starts to say.

The other faerie, Seronel, looks shocked and interrupts him. "Marik! We are not supposed to speak of it. This is...this is treason!"

Marik, gaze still locked firmly on mine, moves quicker than I've ever seen him. I barely have the time to lift my sword to block a hit that doesn't come, and Marik has struck. Seronel's head goes flying, landing in the red dirt and rolling like a basketball. Blue blood spurts from his neck and Zephyr startles to the left as Seronel's body slumps, tumbling as if in slow motion to the ground.

"I followed my orders and found you, Prince Aries," Marik says carefully, wiping the blood from his blade onto his trousers before he sheathes it. "Unfortunately, poor Seronel was killed during our exchange and I was left with no choice but to return his body for Planting."

I understand what he is saying. He is not here to kill me or Rory, not here to drag us back...but to give me a warning. Things in the Sidhe court are more serious than I'd ever imagined.

Marik slides off his horse and grabs Seronel's headless body, flinging it over Orchid's saddle before he climbs up behind it. He doesn't bother grabbing the young faerie's head. I stare at the dead eyes, then look back at Marik with a lifted brow.

He smirks as he explains, "He thought he could replace me. Thought that because he dipped his wick in the Queen's candle, he had some sort of status." Marik's smile fades. "Be careful, Aries. The Queen does not share the entirety of her plans with anyone, not even me, but whatever she's working on...it's big. She's been forcing open Tears and sending scouts through in unheard of numbers. Some of them have been returning with strange things. Some haven't been returning at all. I'd take your little changeling and get as far away as you can. Zephyr should lend you speed. He was always meant to be yours."

Chapter Twenty-Five

Rory

I reach the Dead Wood out of breath, covered in sweat and fighting with my terror. Not fear for me, but for Aries. I know he's an excellent swordsman, or used to be, but as an agent, how much was he able to practice? Even the most skilled fighter could make a deadly mistake.

I should have stayed. Aries is right about my lack of skill with the sword or bow, but I could have asked to borrow one of his daggers. I've had plenty of experience with those living on the streets. Granted, my daggers were flip blades or rusty kitchen knives, but still.

I can't convince myself to go into the Dead Wood without him, so I stand at the edge. The trees that are still standing are ashy and burned, spindly things that look like a good burst of wind would topple them over. There are no leaves, just empty grasping limbs and rotted bark. The air is hazy and when I breathe in deep, I can smell the lingering smoke, bitter as sulfur.

I turn my back, albeit reluctantly, to the trees and stare at the horizon. I know Aries wanted me to find a place to hide but I can't, not until I know it's truly necessary. Instead, I fold my arms over my chest and watch the smudge on the horizon. I can't see what's happening or who is who. My imagination paints pictures of the worst—whatever faerie bastard the Queen sent lopping Aries' head off or running him through with a lance, not even slowing down.

"Stop that, Rory," I scold myself, my voice loud in the otherwise quiet air. "Aries can take care of himself. You'll see…a few minutes and he'll be heading back this way." Honestly, whatever happened between Aries and our pursuers is probably already over, as long as it took me to reach the woods.

The smudge on the horizon is getting bigger with every passing second, and moving faster than even Aries, light on his feet though he may be, could move. My heart starts to race when I see that whoever it is, they are on a horse.

"Shit, *fuck*, goddamn," I curse, awkwardly drawing the sword at my waist. I nearly drop it trying to pull it from the sheath. Aries said to hide, but from the quick look I'd taken into the woods, there was nowhere *to* hide. Sure, I could duck behind a fallen tree and hope for the best, but it wouldn't take much more than luck and a glance to spot me.

If I'm going down, then I plan to go down fighting.

My arm is already shaking from holding the sword. Inside, my monster stirs. I debate letting it loose—I'd definitely have a better chance of surviving with the beast at the helm but who knows where it would take me afterward. I could wake up in an orgy or covered in bodies of a different, less alive kind.

The horse and rider slow as they approach. The light from the suns makes it hard to see details, so I lift my free hand to shade my eyes. I can tell the rider is male from the breadth of his shoulders. He's not a giant or anything, but they are too square for anything but the most masculine woman. And he's Black, which has hope swelling inside me.

Aries is not the only Black faerie in the Sidhe court but he is one of a few.

I lower my sword but don't sheathe it yet, not until Aries—and it definitely is Aries—stops the horse a dozen feet away. Emotion swelling quicker than I can handle, I fumble the sword back into the sheath and run toward him, reaching his side just as Aries slides out of the saddle.

I hit him at a run, arms around his face and face in his neck in seconds. He smells of salt—his sweat—and horse. It's not a pleasant combination but I put up with it because it's *him.*

"Hey, it's okay," Aries soothes, rubbing my back, and rather than being comforting, his words reignite my anger instead.

I step back and swat his arm repeatedly. "Don't *ever* do that again!"

"Do what?" Aries blinks down at me, rubbing his arm. I roll my eyes. I didn't hit him that hard.

"Send me off while you stay behind to play hero! Guess what, Aries? Heroes *die.*" I snap. "If anyone gets to kill you, it's going to be *me.*"

"I'll hold you to that, firebug. Promise to make it hurt?" Aries grins, his teeth shining.

"Guarantee it," I agree. Now that pleasantries are out of the way, I turn to the horse. "Who is this lovely? Reminds me of Nexus."

"He certainly should. He's the finest of his get. Rory, meet Zephyr." Aries pats the tall roan's neck. Zephyr tosses his head, shaking his dark mane.

"Hello, Zephyr." I stroke his soft nose. "What happened back there?" I ask, keeping my eyes on the horse.

"Something odd," Aries answers, and his voice sounds strange.

I meet his gaze. "Oh?"

"It seems we have an ally in the castle. I didn't need to spill a drop of blood and still left with a steed. We'll be able to cover more ground this way," Aries says. I try to feel happy about that. I *should* be happy—the quicker we get to the Unsidhe, the sooner I'll be safe from the Queen's torment.

But it also means the sooner Aries and I will need to part ways. I'm not ready.

"I know faerie steeds are hardy, but I would have thought crossing a desert would be pushing the limits. He hardly looks winded," I muse. "Do you think it safe to take him up the mountain?"

"I would trust Zephyr to carry us to the ends of the world and back if we asked him to," Aries answers. "He can go days without water, weeks without food."

"So," I change the subject, staring off at the empty horizon again. "Our friend in the castle. Did they say why they helped us?"

"Apparently Queen Nuala is fading," Aries says. I'm not surprised, and I can't say I'm disappointed. It certainly explained the Queen's increased libido. The closer she gets to death, the more she'd cling to life. "Apparently, she's planning something. Something that has even her closest allies concerned."

I get a bad feeling in my chest and step back, crossing my arms over my chest. "This ally... It's Marik, isn't it?"

"I know you don't get along," Aries says, sounding sympathetic, and I scoff. That is putting it mildly. He steps forward and lifts his hand to my cheek. "Trust me, I'm just as angry about his part in our separation as you are, but I don't think he's working an angle here."

He doesn't know Marik the way I do, doesn't know the things his friend has done, and I find no reason to enlighten him. I don't want to relive any of those days and I definitely don't want to see pity in his eyes. Or, worse, for him to try to defend the actions of his friend.

"Whatever. He's gone now and we're both still here. We should get a move on." I turn and face the Dead Woods again.

"Rory," Aries says, resting his hand on my shoulder and squeezing. "I'm going to keep you safe. I promise."

The words wrap around me with an invisible weight and I shiver. "You shouldn't make promises you might not be able to keep," I say, a warning he shouldn't have needed.

"I will keep this one." Aries walks in front of me and cups my face. "I will die before I let anyone harm you."

It shouldn't be reassuring, but as we turn to face the Dead Woods, with its creepy trees and shifting shadows...I'm not scared because Aries is at my side.

* * * *

Marik

At Queen Nuala's feet, I kneel, waiting her judgment for my 'mistake'. I adapted long ago to pain and she knows it will not move me. Her hands and whips can only break my skin and bones—my spirit has been numb for ages. With my little rebellion in the desert, I have ensured that the only thing she can hurt me with is outside of her grasp for at least a little longer.

My feelings for my prince may be unrequited but that does not make them any less real. She could tear my heart from my chest by breaking his, a fact she knows well. I suspect it amuses her to toy with me like this. I suspect it is the only reason she has not grown bored of my body.

"What if I lashed you? A hundred—no, a thousand—welts across your spine?" Queen Nuala paces before me, her bare feet striking the stone like thunder.

"As you wish, Your Majesty," I say agreeably. "Would you like me to grab the whip?"

"No! It's no fun when you don't cry," she screeches. Unhinged, that's what she's become. She'd always been violent and manipulative, but she used to be sane.

"I could cry for you, my Queen, if you wish," I offer. I've become an excellent player in her game, twisting myself into whatever piece she needs. A pawn, a rook, a king...at first to survive. Then, once Aodhan fled Faerie on the heels of his little mortal, to fill the aching numbness in my chest. It's time for me to wake up.

Queen Nuala used to be cunning. Now, she is only cruel.

I fear Faerie will not survive her reign much longer. Already, the May-tree is screaming. As she weakens, something else gets stronger...something dark. It is straining against the fabric of our world, struggling to break free. An old god, the trees whisper to me when I walk in their shadows.

I do not know enough of the Queen's plans yet to see the bigger picture, but it grows clearer every day. In her efforts to prolong her own life, she's putting all of Faerie at risk.

Want to see more from this author?
Here's a taster for you to enjoy!

Demon Daddy:
The Faerie Prince's Heart
KD Ellis

Excerpt

Rory

The Dead Woods are exactly as their name suggests—dead. Standing timber, dry as bone, brittle as ash, coated in dark soot and rot. As soon as the desert is out of sight behind us, I crouch and run my fingers through the dirt. It is dry as chalk. Every step we take sends clouds of off-white powder billowing around us. While it irritates my nose and threatens to make me sneeze, it has some benefits. When it settles, drifting slowly down with nary a breeze to bother it, our footsteps are covered. Vanished, as if we never walked here.

"Was there a fire?" I wonder out loud as I follow Aries over a fallen tree. It's so desiccated that it's hard to identify the species. It crumbles beneath my knee when I rest my weight upon it and I nearly fall. Only Aries' hands on my arms keep me upright, steadying me.

"Perhaps," Aries answers. Zephyr stomps his foot and tosses his head. I swear his golden eyes are watching me with jealousy. Aries is slow to release me. Once he does, he pats the horse's neck then continues speaking, "We know little about the Wilds. Few dare to venture here and even fewer return. Those who do… Well, best not to speak of them."

He looks rattled at whatever memories my question has stirred. Goosebumps raise on my flesh, though it is far from cold. I want to press, to search for any hint at what is to come, but I don't want to know what he is thinking of, not when so few of the horrors I'd witnessed have caused him to flinch.

Spiders crawl down my spine. I tamp down the fear.

We walk for ages before I see the first sign of life.

A small, green stalk barely the size of my pinky finger with two limp yellow petals drooping from the white pistil at the center. It should feel hopeful. Instead, it looks sad.

We continue walking. Soon enough, the small sprig is not the only growing thing. As the second sun reaches its zenith, I feel like I've stepped through a looking glass, into a lush rainforest. The air is hot and muggy, and I am grateful for the tall trees with their large fronds that give us shade. The ground is soft and squishy. I lose the shredded fabric protecting my feet quickly as it is sucked into the mud and sticks.

Even the smell is intoxicating. I try to think of a comparison, but nothing is quite right. It is sweeter than strawberries, crisper than a fresh cut apple. It sends my stomach rumbling. I've barely pressed my hand to my abdomen to quiet it when I see the fruit tree.

Golden orbs dangle from the tree branches, each one the size of my fist and lightly glowing. I take a step toward them. Then Aries grips my arm tight, stopping me in my tracks.

I bare my teeth as I spin to face him, hunger overriding everything else. My jaws ache, a telltale sign that my mouth is full of daggers. Would I prefer meat? Of course. There is nothing like smoked jackrabbit to fill a belly, but right now the mysterious fruit smells better even than that.

Aries' eyes widen slightly but he doesn't let go, not even in the face of my monster. His skin is cold against mine. "Rory…" he says, voice trailing off as I growl.

"Hungry," my monster speaks with my mouth. I taste copper on my tongue.

"I don't like the look of them," Aries answers. How brave he is, to contradict my beast with his teeth out.

"I don't like the look of you," my monster says, ever a rebellious teenager, but the mulish answer is enough for me to regain control of my mouth. Pulpy silver needles fall to the dirt. I lift my hand to my throbbing face.

Aries looks wary, his hand slow as he extends it toward me. "We should keep moving."

I allow him to lead me away but I can't resist looking over my shoulder. The once-golden orbs are now cloying gray-and-red, sticky with mucus and lumpy with fat. They spasm weakly in time with my heartbeat. Each shuddering pulse sends off-white slime leaking down the moist flesh.

They still smell sweet.

I turn my face away.

I do not thank Aries for his intervention, though I know not what he saved me from. I fear I can guess. Here, near the base of a willow weeping salt, I see a cage of bone. Nestled within is an inflorescence of white orchids.

There, by a craggy boulder, is a spray of knucklebones.

Aries' hand tightens on mine and I let him draw me closer to his side. To make him feel better, of course, not because I am afraid.

* * * *

Dusk falls but we keep walking, until my soles feel shredded and it's a miracle I'm not leaving bloody footprints behind. I'm determined not to slow us down, and in truth, it is Zephyr who stops us.

As we reach a stream, the water flowing dark and oily, Zephyr rears. He tosses his head, his loud whinny splitting open the night. Aries grabs his reins and I watch, breath bated, as he struggles to restrain him. Foam flies from the horse's maw. I shouldn't notice, the timing is terrible, but I can't help but see how Aries' muscles cord and bulge, his skin glistening.

Then Zephyr lands one of his dinner-plate hooves on Aries chest and sends him flying—right into the oil-slick river. He sinks slowly, as if in quicksand, and I am moving without thought.

On my knees on the bank, I sink my hands, now tipped with curving claws, into the sickeningly thick warm water until they snag on something fabric. I drag him out, coughing and sputtering, barely noticing the large gouges my nails have left in his chest and arms. I am too busy pounding his back as he vomits sludge.

Only once he draws in his first ragged breath do I have time to feel guilty at the blue blood staining his skin. It is enough for me to shed my claws, leaving behind raw red fingertips in their place.

"Zephyr," Aries says, gaze pained as he stares at the empty stretch of grass where the horse once stood.

While I'd been dragging Aries from the river, the horse must have fled. Should I feel bad for not prioritizing the horse? Would Aries, being a faerie, have been able to survive in the dark water while I restrained Zephyr? *Could* I have restrained him, even if I tried?

"If he is anything like Nexus," I say, speaking of his sire, "he will find his way back to us on his own."

"I hope you are right." Aries' voice breaks. There is more emotion in him now for Zephyr than I've ever heard from him for me. It turns me to stone while breaking me into pieces.

I push myself to my feet and hesitate before I hold my hand out to Aries. He takes it as if nothing is wrong and allows me to pull him to standing.

I want to cry, for myself and the things that could have been if he was a different person, if *I* was a different person. To let my anger strike him for the injustice of his worry for a horse that he's rarely shown for me.

"We should not cross this water in the dark," is all I say instead. My forearms itch where I submerged them, skin writhing as if bugs have crawled beneath it.

Aries stands statue still, but his shadow, cast from the dim moonlight filtering through the canopy above us, sways from side to side. I lift my gaze to Aries' eyes and they are black, pupils blown.

He allows me to lead him farther up the banks, away from the water and towards an uprooted tree. I guide Aries into the exposed cradle knoll. He is compliant— too compliant to be natural. I am suddenly reminded of the Gravel Girls. The synthetic salts were introduced to treat severe arthritis.

I don't know who discovered that chewing it gave users a heroin high without the coming down, or how desperate they must have been to try it. I will never forget the sight of their paper-thin skin and broken teeth, or their chemical-born haunted happiness.

I can only hope that whatever magic the water held, it releases Aries quickly. As he sinks into the dirt depression, his antlers catch briefly in the exposed root system. The weedy, tentacle-like vines knot around the spines and hold him in place, a nature made bondage. Old resentment urges me to leave him tangled. It will still be nothing like the suffering I've felt at his hands or by his orders.

I start untying the curling roots anyway. One antler is freed and the second nearly so when Aries moans. I freeze, fingers going still, as he meets my gaze. Without thinking, I had straddled his waist to reach his surroyal tines. Now I can feel his manhood between my thighs.

I leave him caught in the vines as I scramble off him, heat flooding my face.

"Ruari," Aries moans my old name, his voice broken and breathy. "I need you. Come to me as you once did." His voice sounds lucid but sweat beads along his brow above his glassy eyes.

"Never that," I murmur. If I allow him to take me again, to claim my body fully with his, it will never again be like it was. We will come together as equals or nothing. "Sleep, Aries. You are not yourself."

"I am more myself than I have ever been," Aries argues. His hands, not bound by anything, lower to the closure of his trousers. I suck in a breath to tell him to stop but he is too quick for me. That, or maybe I don't want it badly enough.

His erection is engorged and leaking.

Is it the effects of the water? I was immersed up to my shoulders and all I feel is itchy. But I was careful not to swallow the greasy slick, and he drank enough to drown a horse.

"Come to me, Ruari," Aries repeats his plea, his slender fingers wrapping around the root of his cock. "I am burning."

"You are drunk," I scold him. Drunk or drugged, there is little difference. Perhaps it would be fair play to repay him for the wrongs that have been done unto me, yet I cannot stomach the thought. Stealing from him what was taken from me will not return it.

"Look, Ruari. I weep for you." He trails his fingers through his pre-cum, then holds out them out. They shine in starlight. I drop my gaze, cheeks aflame.

"Then weep alone."

It is a long night. Aries pleads for me in between pleasuring himself and I lose count of the number of times that he spills. His poor cock must be chafed and raw but still at first dawn, he is begging, his hand on his shaft and his eyes on me. Finally, as second dawn crests, his words slow. His body grows sluggish and sleep takes him.

I am left, untouched but yearning, to keep watch into the day.

About the Author

KD Ellis is a queer author of M/M+ romances. They enjoy crafting stories with a bit of angst, a dollop of darkness and always a happy ending! They/them

KD Ellis loves to hear from readers. You can find their contact information, website details and author profile page at https://www.firstforromance.com/

PUBLISHING

Sign up for our newsletter and find out about all our
romance book releases, eBook sales and promotions,
sneak peeks and FREE romance books!

www.ingramcontent.com/pod-product-compliance
Lightning Source LLC
Chambersburg PA
CBHW050531260626
47157CB00004B/1555